Samantha Alexander .... colnshire with a variety of animals including her thoroughbred horse, Bunny, and her two kittens, Cedric and Bramble. Her schedule is almost as busy and exciting as her plots – she writes a number of columns for newspapers and magazines, is a teenage agony aunt for BBC Radio Leeds and in her spare time she regularly competes in dressage and showjumping.

Books by Samantha Alexander available from Macmillan

RIDING SCHOOL

HOLLYWELL STABLES

RIDING SCHOOL

2
Emma

SAMANTHA ALEXANDER

MACMILLAN CHILDREN'S BOOKS

First published 1999 by Macmillan Children's Books
a division of Macmillan Publishers Ltd
25 Eccleston Place, London SW1W 9NF
Basingstoke and Oxford
www.macmillan.co.uk
Associated companies throughout the world

ISBN 0 330 36837 0

A CIP catalogue record for this book is available from
the British Library.

Phototypeset by Intype London Limited
Printed and bound in Great Britain by
Mackays of Chatham plc, Chatham, Kent

Samantha Alexander and Macmillan Children's Books would like to thank all at Suzanne's Riding School, especially Suzanne Marczak.

Chapter One

"I heard him on the phone," insisted Steph, wringing her hands in despair. "He was telling his mother that she was the most fantastic girl he'd ever clapped eyes on, with a brilliant personality and just what he'd been looking for all his life."

"Are you sure he was talking about a woman?" said Kate.

"Well who do you think he was talking about, the prime minister?" Steph paced up and down, getting more and more irate. "Anyway, he's been wearing a new aftershave lately, that says it all."

"Oh big deal." Kate folded her arms. "Good detective work, Sherlock."

"Just because he's our riding instructor, doesn't mean he has to be a monk," Rachel pointed out.

I was sitting at the table writing out pony care fact sheets in an effort to swot up for the riding school stable management certificate.

We'd officially formed what we called the "Six Pack" at the start of the summer holidays. Six horse-mad girls all dedicated to Brook House

Riding School which had very nearly closed down. Sophie's dad had stepped in at the last moment as a silent partner and saved the school and the horses. Since then Brook House had gone from strength to strength and we all dedicated our weekends and every spare moment to helping out with the ponies and improving our riding. Sophie was really nice, Jodie quite serious, Rachel shy, Kate bossy and Steph moody, but we all had one thing in common – Horses!

"You don't get it, do you?" Steph raised her arms in alarm. "If Guy falls in love there'll be no special evening lessons or picnics or quizzes or pony weeks. He'll be too busy going out on dates – he won't have time for us!"

Real concern flickered over everyone's faces. All the Six Pack helped out at weekends and holidays and in return were often given a free lesson from Guy. We'd all got used to hogging his time; we'd had him all to ourselves for five weeks and our riding had come on in leaps and bounds. Without Guy's energy and enthusiasm, Brook House would revert back to being just an ordinary riding school instead of something dynamic and special.

"We've got to do something," Sophie muttered.

"It's for his own good," nodded Kate.

"And for Brook House, and for his showjumping career," said Rachel.

"And for the horses," I added, thinking as always of our four-legged friends.

"We don't have a choice." Sophie chased away any doubts. We all nodded.

"Only nineteen hours to go!" Rachel burst into the horsy saloon where we hung out between lessons and chores, looking as if she was about to explode with excitement.

Own a Pony Week had been Guy's idea and had proved a sell-out success. Basically each person had a pony to look after for the whole week which involved grooming, feeding, mucking out and riding. There were loads of activities planned such as group lessons, hacks, a treasure hunt, cross country, polo and even ice skating one evening. It was just the most happening event ever. I'd got my name down first and booked Buzby, my favourite riding school pony. Owning him for a week was going to be incredible. And it all started at nine tomorrow morning.

I slipped into Buzby's stable where he was tacked up waiting for the next ride. He was a gorgeous dapple grey. He was cheeky and mischievous but I loved him to bits and spent all my spare time looking after him and pretending he was mine. Now it was really going to happen, at least for one week.

I rummaged through my new grooming box which had taken me ages to save up for and pulled out the "cactus cloth" which was supposed to make stable stains miraculously disappear. Buzby scowled, knotting his woolly brows together in disapproval.

Guy wasn't just an ordinary riding instructor. He was a showjumper with two Dutch warmblood horses and his ambition was to ride for England one day. Even Kate, who was scared of jumping, had improved beyond all recognition.

It was our ambition for Brook House to be voted Riding School of the Year but we all knew we had heaps of improving to do before then. I bent down and brushed out Buzby's fetlocks which seemed to act as magnets for bits of dried mud.

"Where's Steph?" Sophie popped her head over the door, looking harassed. "She's wanted pronto in the arena."

I shrugged. Steph was really good at disappearing when there was work to be done.

"OK," I groaned, "I'll try and find her." There was no way I was going to do Steph's chores for her, especially the lead rein class. I checked the saloon and then went to see if she was with her grey pony, Monty.

I eventually tracked her down in the office where she was bent over the desk.

"You creep," I howled, after peering over her right shoulder.

"Get lost, Emma." She spun round, eyes blazing, and stuffed the half wrapped present inside her jacket pocket. "It's nothing to do with you."

It was Guy's birthday today and I'd bought him a pencil with a horsy rubber and made a carrot and mint cake for his horses, although Buzby had already devoured half of it. We all knew that Steph had a crush on Guy but now it stood out a mile – she'd bought him a pair of leather riding gloves which must have cost a bomb.

I danced around the office tormenting her until she turned bright red.

"Ouch." She came up behind me and yanked at my hair.

"That'll teach you to grow up." She could be so spiteful. "You can be such a baby, Emma. At least I don't play with model horses and pretend to ride broomsticks. At least boys like me. You'll never get a boyfriend the way you behave."

"You snake!" I squeaked, really stung. I reeled back and desperately tried to think of something to say. I knew I'd regret it as soon as the words tumbled out.

"Well that's where you're wrong," I croaked, "because boys do like me. In fact, as a matter of fact . . ." I floundered but couldn't stop myself. " . . . I've got a boyfriend."

Steph gaped and then opened and shut her mouth in shock. A wave of triumph swept over me when I saw her lost for words.

"You're kidding."

"I am not! His name's Craig and he's horse-mad and he thinks Buzby's the best pony in the world."

"Well then he must be a fool." Steph raised an eyebrow, unsure what to think.

I really did have a pen pal called Craig who was coming to Brook House for Own a Pony Week but I'd never met him face to face before.

"Well you'll be able to judge for yourself," I snapped back, digging myself a ten foot hole, "because he's coming here tomorrow – and he's staying the whole week!"

Chapter Two

"Emma, breakfast!" Mum bellowed up through the floorboards.

I always believe that if you blank something out of your mind then somehow it will go away or at least not turn out half as bad. So on the morning of Own a Pony Week I leapt out of bed, revelling in the thrill of looking after Buzby for a whole week and not giving Craig or Guy a second thought.

Mickey, my pet hamster, irritated that I'd been up for two minutes without noticing him, raced frantically on his wheel for thirty seconds, leapt off and flipped over the lego jumps I'd set up in his cage. I gave him his Happy Hamster treat which had become a morning ritual and pulled on my best jods and yellow riding shirt. Grabbing my riding hat, I ran onto the landing, and clinging to the banister, pretended the stairs were a cross-country complex at Badminton.

Dad was in his special chair, not reading his paper for once. Mum was wearing her anxious look which said, "I've got to support your dad so please understand." Something was definitely up.

"Now, Emma, about this pony week." Dad's glasses always steamed up when he drank his tea. I tried not to smile. "We've spent a lot of money at that riding school this year and it seems to us all you've learnt is how to have your head in the clouds. You're still in the same riding group that you were in at the start of the year."

"Yes, but Dad—"

"I don't want to hear your excuses, Emma. I'm not paying out for special riding courses if all you're going to do is muck about with your friends."

"But I don't," I protested, a lump of panic rising in my throat.

"Your mum and I, well we've decided, that if you don't pass the certificate for this pony week, well . . . we're going to have to reconsider your weekly lessons."

"What?" I fell forward on my chair which I'd been rocking back. "But you can't." I looked at Mum pleadingly but she buried her head in the fridge.

"Anyway, it'd be a good thing if you took up another sport – it's not as if we'll ever be able to buy you a pony. What about netball or gymnastics – there are other things apart from riding."

"There are *not*!" I yelled, knowing I shouldn't really answer back, but unable to stop myself. "Riding is everything. Without ponies I'd shrivel up and die."

"Now, Emma, you're being dramatic." Dad shuffled awkwardly.

"*I am not.*" I could feel my face going crimson. "If you take me away from Brook House, I'll never speak to you again. Not ever. And I'll stop eating. I'll go on a fast."

Dad smiled as if that was funny and I burst into tears, huge racking sobs that startled even me. As a baby I'd been able to sob for England and I obviously hadn't lost the knack.

"I hate you." I drew back, gasping from the shock of what I'd just said, feeling as if someone had slapped me across the face. Then I grabbed my bag and bolted for the door, unable to look at their wounded faces.

Mum and Dad had adopted me when I was three years old and had been fantastic parents ever since. I knew they tried to afford as much as they could and it wasn't always easy. I felt terrible about what I'd said. The bus was five minutes late so I dived into the newsagent's and bought two Mars Bars, a Bounty and some Chocolate Buttons.

The car had to beep three times before I registered

Sophie hanging out of the window. I usually had a lift with Rachel but she was at the dentist.

"Why didn't you tell me you needed a lift?" Sophie homed in on my face and the chocolate bulging out of my pockets. Mr Green eased the expensive Jaguar out of the bus lane and pretended not to notice that I'd been crying. Sophie immediately squeezed my hand. We had a rule in the Six Pack that we would all be there for each other, through thick and thin, and although we had our squabbles, when it really counted we didn't let each other down.

"We'll talk about it at the stables," Sophie whispered and I felt the frantic beating in my chest beginning to ease. Sophie was the nicest person I'd ever met and even though her dad was rich she was normal and down to earth and never once showed off. All her thoughts were always for other people.

"There's only one thing you can do," said Sophie. We were sitting on a straw bale in the barn. It was the only private place we could find – the yard was buzzing. "You've got to pass the stable management certificate."

"You don't understand," I hissed at Sophie, trying to keep the tremble out of my voice. "You're talking to the person who only got three per cent in her last school exam."

"But this is different – it's assessed on the whole week, and it's about horses."

"Sophie, you're not listening. You're a brain, I never remember anything. I'm thick."

"You are not, you just panic. Now have faith. You can do it, I'll help you." Sophie put an arm round my shoulder but I still felt completely hopeless.

"Emma Parker?" Guy called out my name and I went up to get my special badge and schedule for the week. The saloon was milling with people and the Six Pack had resorted to sitting on top of the table we usually reserved for cleaning tack.

There was no sign of Craig. I remembered seeing his picture in *In the Saddle* and it was his carrot-red hair that had first drawn me to him. I thought he looked interesting and good fun.

"Rachel Banks? Jessica Friar?" Every pony at the riding school had been booked apart from Elvis and Faldo, two New Forest ponies who had only just been broken in. Rachel came back with her badge marked Rusty – her favourite pony. Guy explained that today we were going to ride in the school so that everybody could get used to their ponies.

11

A whoop went up from the front when Guy confirmed that the last day was cross-country with a professional photographer coming in to take pictures of everyone jumping, free of charge. Despite everything, a flame of excitement was lighting up in my stomach. This was it! We'd all thought of nothing else for weeks. Various instructions followed, for example no running round the stables, keeping the muck heap tidy, no leaving gates open and everybody being responsible for their own belongings.

I was just beginning to breathe a sigh of relief that I'd got off scot-free, when the western-style louvred doors flew back on their hinges and Craig stumbled in, mumbling some apology about getting up late, his red face matching his hair.

I was so embarrassed, I couldn't look up. Craig pushed forward and grabbed the only available chair, which was Guy's, then winked at me and mouthed hello. I smiled back woodenly and cursed Steph who was thumping her chest, imitating a beating heart. I barely heard the rest of Guy's instructions and suddenly decided this was the worst day of my life. And it wasn't going to get any better.

"He's awful!" Kate rode up on Archie. "What on earth do you see in him?"

12

You could always rely on friends to be honest.

There were three other boys on pony week but they were all quiet and normal. In Craig's letters he said he could ride but there was no evidence of it in the school. His reins were up round his chin and his feet rammed back in the stirrups. Guy was trying to instruct us but Craig was keeping a one-way conversation going with Sophie.

After half an hour he had fallen off twice but the worst thing was that he was doing it deliberately to show off in front of Sophie. Guy seemed to be getting really annoyed and I felt he was blaming me. The more worried I got the more nervous I became and my riding deteriorated. I lost all my coordination and Buzby ploughed into a holly bush which scratched me all down the side of my face.

"You OK?" Rachel kicked forward on Rusty. "There are too many riders on the arena," she whispered. "Guy should have separated us into two groups."

"As nearly everybody seems to have bonded with their ponies, I'd like to move on to canter." Guy paced up and down in front of a pair of jump wings.

"Oh cripes." Rachel snuck back into her position, two rides behind.

"If he carries on riding this badly, he'll kill

13

himself." Steph trotted past on Monty looking bemused. "Do something, Emma, he's your boyfriend." Softening just a little, I remembered how I used to talk non-stop in riding lessons because I was so nervous. Craig was probably acting the fool for the same reason.

"If you just sit back and push your heel down you'll find it a lot easier to stay on," I said, riding up to him and putting on my friendliest smile.

He wrinkled up his freckled face as if he was going to crack a joke. Then, like a viper, he spat out, "Shut up, fatso, I don't need your help."

Two girls in the line tittered but Guy was up at the other end and didn't hear, thank goodness. I felt mortified, as if this awful boy had just viciously squeezed my heart and wrung the life out of it. Nobody had ever referred to my weight before, at least not to my face. I could feel hot colour sweeping up my neck. My chest felt tight. I had to get away. Out of the arena. I couldn't stem the tears that were welling up.

"Emma Parker, where are you going?" Guy was always really strict on his lessons and we respected him for it.

"Buz, walk on!" I thumped my heels into Buzby's sides but he wouldn't budge. I felt as if my cheeks were going to burst into flame. Gradually the whole ride were pulling up and staring.

14

"Get on!" I flapped the reins in vain and then in desperation raised my crop and tapped Buz down the shoulder. Squealing with indignation he flattened his ears and arched his back in a stilted buck. I could feel Craig's mocking eyes boring into me and everybody else's too.

"Emma, what's the matter?" Sophie was suddenly there on Rocket, the picture of concern.

I couldn't stand it any more. I was whirring with humiliation.

"Just leave it," I mumbled and jumped off Buz. I fled to the saloon, racking sobs breaking loose as soon as I was through the doors. At that moment it wasn't Craig I hated, or the girls who had giggled, it was me – for being so thick and stupid. I stared down at my round, fleshy arms and angrily pinched the loose skin until a vivid red mark flared up.

"Emma?"

My head jerked up in alarm. "Jodie!" I couldn't believe she was sitting there, as large as life. "But you're supposed to be in India!" A lovely warm surge of comfort ran through me. Good, solid, practical Jodie who had a solution for everything. She was at my side in seconds, hugging me and passing me endless tissues.

"Mum and I came home early because Dad had

to work all the time and I was missing Minstrel so much I felt ill."

She'd had her hair cut which made her look more grown-up and she was in new clothes which showed off her skinny figure. "You look wonderful," I croaked, tears still streaming down my face. "I'm s-so glad you're back."

"Me too." She grasped my hands and stared pointedly into my swollen eyes. "But Em, you've got to tell me, what's happened to get you into this state?"

Chapter Three

"These are nags, not quality horses," snapped the girl, turning on her heel and clipping past Frank's stable. "Where's the owner? I'm not going to be ripped off."

She'd appeared from nowhere in a flashy sports car without an appointment and had demanded to be shown the horses. She was every riding school's worst nightmare. She had big loop earrings and high heels and thought she knew everything. We weren't supposed to be rude to customers, but she wasn't a horse lover – it stood out a mile.

Guy was having a meeting in the house with the owner, Mrs Brentford, the full-time groom, Sandra, and Sophie's dad. Everyone else was having lunch in the saloon and playing charades. I'd sneaked out to give Buzby a coconut slice and check his water.

"This is Ebony Jane." I introduced the gorgeous bay horse in the next stable. She was an ex-race-horse with a sweet nature, and was one of the most popular horses at the riding school. She was old now, with weak hocks which prevented her from jumping, but she was safe and trustworthy and had taught hundreds of people to ride.

"Ebby won a race once, a handicap. There's a picture of her in the tack room." I kissed her soft nose and then stood on the hinge of the door to undo her head collar.

"OK, I don't want the dinosaur's history." The girl's face crumpled as if she'd just eaten something distasteful. "Have you got anything better?"

"But Ebby's lovely," I protested. "She's kind and gentle and wouldn't hurt a fly." The words poured out but she wasn't even listening. She'd moved on to the next stable where her critical eyes were greedily devouring Minstrel.

"Now this looks more like it," she said. The stunning chestnut Arab glanced across from his hay net, snorted, then went back to the more serious matter of eating.

"He's not in the riding school," I informed her, with great pleasure.

"This is the one I'm riding," she claimed, completely ignoring me and rushing forward to draw back the bolt on the stable door.

"He's not on offer." Jodie's voice was hard and brittle behind me.

The girl stopped in her tracks and swivelled round, her lips parted.

"As Emma's just told you, he's not a riding school horse."

She glanced sideways as if noticing me for the first time. Then she weighed up Jodie. After a brief silence she seemed to accept the situation.

"Fair enough," she said, her interest in Minstrel fizzling out in a flash. For a second I felt envious of Jodie for the way she could handle grown-ups at the age of twelve – only a year older than me.

"Perhaps you could tell me where I could find Guy Marshall?"

"Right here." Jodie pointed to where Guy was striding out of the house, looking intently at the girl, his face splitting into a wide grin. It was so unlike Guy because usually he hated undesirable clients. I tried to knot my brows together to warn him that she was trouble.

"I thought you'd got lost," he almost gasped, holding out a sun-browned hand and clasping hers. Jodie and I exchanged looks of confusion. Guy never behaved like this.

"It seems your little pupils don't follow the celebrities like they used to." The girl stepped nearer to Guy as if she was sharing a private joke with him. Then she looked pointedly at us, her tawny, oval eyes glittering with amusement. "You see, girls," she said flicking back her oat-blond hair, "I'm Cindy Morell. And if you've read any pony magazines lately you'll know that I'm a famous eventer."

"Cindy Morell was here and you didn't recognize her?" Steph's voice was stony with shock. She was pressed up against the saloon window with Kate and Sophie, in the vain hope that Cindy might return that afternoon and they could get her autograph.

"Well, she kind of looked different without her riding gear," I mumbled, feeling quite important since I'd been the first to meet her. Not only was she a famous eventer, but she was romantically linked with a vet from the fab TV series *Animal Kingdom* which I watched religiously every week.

"So why does somebody like that want to hire a riding school horse?" Rachel was sitting at the table showing the least enthusiasm.

"Because she's up here staying with relatives and she wants a horse to ride." Kate rolled her eyes as if Rachel was stupid.

"There's got to be more to it than that," said Rachel screwing up her elflike face. "Haven't any of you considered for one second that she might be the mystery girlfriend?"

Steph's jaw dropped. Kate let out a low groan. Jodie, who had been writing her diary, looked up with total indifference. "I don't know why you're all so star-struck," she grumbled. "And you, Emma, know as well as I do that Cindy Morell is ambitious and mean. And if Guy does get involved with her she'll eat him for breakfast."

I blushed uncomfortably, knowing full well that I'd turned a blind eye to Cindy's behaviour since I'd found out that she was famous.

"Oh no!" Steph turned from the window, a hand flying up to her mouth. "It's Guy, he's seen us, and he's coming across – he looks furious."

"Well, for once we haven't done anything wrong," Jodie said and carried on writing.

Steph and Kate looked at each other, the colour draining from their faces. "W-we kind of left a load of magazines open in the office about how relationships can ruin your life."

"Oh great, girls, full marks for subtlety," said Jodie, wincing.

We could hear Guy's footsteps approaching. "Quick!" whispered Kate, and we all dived for the horsy manuals on the table and started reading, regardless of the fact that every book was upside down.

"Look, I'm sorry, OK? I didn't realize you'd get that upset." Craig hovered in the doorway of Buzby's stable, awkwardly shuffling his feet. "At

21

my riding school we're always calling each other names, but it doesn't mean anything."

In the half-light of the stable he almost looked genuine. He swallowed hard, rubbing his hand up his neck nervously, and again repeated, "I – I didn't mean it."

Buzby stepped backwards so I couldn't hide behind his shoulder any longer. Feeling exposed, I fixed my eyes on the far manger, humiliation colouring my cheeks for the second time. I'd never forget those girls tittering.

"Look, I can't be that bad – Buzby likes me." Craig shot me a look of appeal as Buzby started licking his outstretched hand. Trust Buz to betray me.

"Can't we be friends?" He deliberately softened his voice. "For Buzby's sake at least." I had to admit, when Craig was being nice he did have a certain charm.

"Look! Up there!" He pointed sharply at the rafters. I'd looked up before I even realized. "Got you!" He had his head cocked to one side and a smile playing on his lips. Before I could stop myself I was smiling back.

"That's better," he said, patting Buzby's nose.

"If you like I could show you all the horses in the yard and we could pair up for the treasure hunt tomorrow," I offered.

22

The smile slipped from Craig's face. "Listen," he said changing the subject, "if that Marshall bloke asks, we're the best of friends, OK?"

I nodded mutely as he backed out of the stable. "If you need any help . . ." I shouted, but he didn't answer.

"My, my." Steph popped her head round the door, grinning triumphantly and clutching the big yard brush in front of her. She made no secret of the fact that she'd been listening behind the door. "We're getting very pally, aren't we? I thought you hated his guts?"

"That was this morning," I said, pulling a face. "Anyway, it was a misunderstanding."

"Puh. I've never seen you so upset."

"Steph, can't you go back to your sweeping or something? Or better still, go trample on the muck heap."

"What's the matter?" Sophie came over, weighed down with two saddles and countless bridles that she was carting back to the tack room.

"Craig's apologized and now Emma's in love again."

"No I am not!" I snapped, all uptight.

"Oh Em." Sophie dropped her load and looked at me as if I were weak in the head. "Don't forgive too easily. You always see everyone through rose-coloured spectacles."

23

"Excuse me?" I raised my voice indignantly.

A blue car swung into the drive and pulled up on the grass verge near the barn. It was Mum and Dad. My heart somersaulted and landed somewhere near my knees. "If anyone's got some apologizing to do, it's me," I groaned. And leaving them to it, I walked across the yard rehearsing what I was going to say for the hundredth time that day.

"I'm sorry," I said. Guy was absolutely livid. My eyes filled with tears and I wanted to put my hands over my mouth to stop myself from sobbing.

I had arrived at the stable the next morning to find that someone had left the pitchfork in Buzby's stable and the lid off the feed bin full of the coarse mix that was kept especially for him.

"Have you any idea what could have happened if he'd stood on that pitchfork?" Guy asked.

I nodded, hardly able to breathe for the knot of fear in my chest. It was too unbearable to even think about it.

"The whole idea of pony week is that you are responsible for your own pony. You were the last in his stable." Guy was speaking extra-slowly as if to emphasize each word.

I remembered quite clearly bedding Buz down and filling up his water. I *couldn't* have left the fork in the stable – I'd never done anything like that in my life. I was always so careful. But no matter how much I tried, I couldn't actually remember putting the pitchfork back in the feed room. I'd been thrown first by Craig, and then by Mum and Dad arriving.

"And then there's the feed bins." Guy sank back in the swivel chair, looking tired and drawn. "How many times have I told you girls to replace the lids?"

"L-lots," I stammered, feeling worse than I'd ever felt in my life.

"If vermin get to the food, they can spread infection. I expected better of you, Emma. I know how much you love that pony."

My eyes welled up and the floor became a blur.

"Had it been anybody else, I'd have sent them packing." said Guy. "Anyway, let this be the end of it. But I don't want to have to call you back in here." There was more than a hint of warning in his voice. "If you want a certificate at the end of the week it's got to be flying colours from now on. I can't give you preferential treatment."

"No. Thanks." I stumbled out of the door in a daze.

"It could have happened to anybody." Rachel was trying her best to make me feel better. All the Six

Pack were being ultra-supportive but I still felt like the most useless person in the world. At least I wasn't the only person to get told off that morning. Someone had left a dismantled bridle on the radiator to dry.

Rachel got two star points for the tidiest stable and the cleanest grooming kit. I tried not to feel too jealous. At least Buzby had done well in the showjumping. Guy had set up a "Chase me Charlie" where the jump gradually gets higher and riders are knocked out if they have a refusal or four faults. Although Buzby was one-paced and tended to jump in slow motion, he was really careful and snapped up his front legs.

When the jump was at two foot nine with a spread there was just Steph, Craig and myself left in. Craig, as if by magic, had suddenly started riding properly.

"As you seem to have miraculously discovered the art of riding, perhaps you could go first?" Guy smiled tightly at Craig, well aware that up to now he'd just been larking about.

"Good luck." I grinned at him as Foxy sidled towards the jump, swishing her tail. Craig was riding on a really short rein, kicking her forward with grim determination. She flew over the jump like a gazelle, but clipped the left wing. The top pole rolled, wavered and then tipped off, flopping on to the soft sand.

"You should have used more left leg," Guy called. "And slower, much slower, it's not a race."

A few minutes later Steph turned bright red when Monty ground to a halt in front of the red and white poles.

"OK, Emma, you're next."

I wheeled Buzby round and kicked extra-hard to get him away from the other ponies. Remembering everything that Guy had taught us I clamped my legs round his sides and kept them there all the way to the jump. Buzby saw a good stride and lengthened, grunting with the effort. All the other ponies, including Minstrel, had got over-excited at repeating the same jump and made mistakes, but Buz only ever got excited about food.

"Come on, boy." This was his chance to shine. I forgot how scared I was and squeezed harder, snapping my eyes shut as he launched himself upwards. "Go on! Go on!"

Kate dropped her reins and started clapping like mad. Buz shot off round the arena, as startled as everyone else. The poles were still in their cups. He'd given it a good, wide berth.

"You brilliant, gorgeous, wonderful pony." I collapsed on his neck, hugging him to death, kissing his spiky mane.

27

"Well done." Steph rode up, a forced smile on her face. "You'd think your boyfriend would at least have congratulated you," she taunted in a thin voice.

"And I suppose you aren't peeved in the slightest?" Kate rode past, arching her eyebrows at Steph, who we all knew liked to be the best at everything.

"Oh Steph, lay off. You've just got the hump because you lost." Sophie flicked a bread roll at Steph and got a reprimanding look from Guy across the room. The saloon had been turned into a dinner hall with long trestle-tables and wooden chairs, and Mrs Brentford and Sandra were serving up hot chicken curry, jacket potatoes or vegetarian chilli.

Steph was laying into me relentlessly about Craig sitting at another table.

"Well can you blame him? The Six Pack are pretty formidable." Rachel grabbed her glass of water after testing the chicken curry. "What's in that?" she gasped.

"Kangaroo meat," Steph answered, peering at the other table over her shoulder. There were four boys and eleven girls on pony week and everyone seemed to have split off into groups.

"The girl with the long plait fancies Craig,"

Steph whispered dramatically, covering her mouth with her hand. "Watch out, Em."

It was as if she knew I was hiding something. I shuffled uneasily, my conscience pricking me more and more. I was just about to change the subject to the treasure hunt which was starting at two o'clock when Guy came across with two orange rosettes, handing one to Rachel and the other to me. In the middle was printed Brook House Riding School: Special Achievement. It was fantastic. It was a life-saver. When my parents saw this they'd have to let me carry on riding.

"Well done, Em," said Sophie, obviously sensing the relief I felt.

"Well aren't you going to show your boyfriend?" Steph's voice grated, oozing resentment.

"There's something I've got to tell you," I blurted out, my conscience finally winning. "Craig's not my boyfriend. I lied. He's my pen pal and until yesterday. I'd only seen his photograph. We hardly know each other."

Silence. Steph glowed with smugness. "I knew it, I just knew it."

Kate looked thunderous. There was a rule in the Six Pack about being totally honest with one another.

"It's all right, Em, don't worry," Sophie reassured me, but even she sounded wounded.

"No it's not!" Kate leapt up, scraping back her chair. "I got chucked out of the Six Pack for telling lies – you can't just ignore it."

"Your case was very different," Jodie mumbled.

"No it wasn't. A lie is a lie. And I think it stinks." She stalked off causing everyone to glance across with casual interest.

"She'll come round." Sophie grimaced, pursing her lips.

"Yeah," said Rachel trying to ease the awkwardness.

Gradually, one by one, they all got up and left, leaving me sitting there on my own, staring at a huge plate of chilli. I looked up at Craig's table. He had his back to me, but the girl with the long plait stared back. She was one of the girls who had tittered the first day in the arena. My face flushed and I was about to look away when she puffed out her cheeks, making fun of my weight. I jerked my head away. And for the first time in my life, I skipped lunch and left the table.

Chapter Four

"A feather, a fir cone, a hoof pick, a ball of lambswool? Is this for real?" Sophie screwed up her nose as she scanned the list.

> A pair of odd socks
> A lead rope
> A chocolate egg
> A strand of horse hair
> A rubber band

"They're easy." Kate snatched the list from Sophie, running her finger impatiently down the page. "Oh cripes, these are the difficult ones." She read aloud, slowly for emphasis: "A golf ball, a round white stone, a four-leaf clover!"

"Look, there are clues," said Jodie, trying to read upside down. "They must have hidden things deliberately."

"Not a four-leaf clover," Kate scoffed. "I've never even seen one."

"They could be plastic," Sophie suggested sensibly.

"Now listen up everybody," said Guy walking round with a clipboard. "I want you all to split up into groups of three and you'll be started off at ten-minute intervals. You've got three hours to find as many treasures as you can. There are twenty items altogether, some more difficult than others. The route is all mapped out for you and you are not to stray from the designated trail. Is that clear?"

"Yes, Mr Marshall."

"There'll be refreshments back at the stables for when you finish, which must be within three hours or you'll be eliminated. Each team must work together and stay together. There's a set of saddle-bags for one member of each team which can be used for carrying the treasure and soft drinks and snacks, but remember, no glass bottles or containers. Are there any questions?"

Kate shot up her hand. "Can we pick our own teams?"

"I don't see why not, providing there's no squabbling."

"I bag Steph and Sophie." Kate glared at me, making her feelings quite plain.

"That leaves Rachel, Jodie and Emma." Sophie stated the obvious.

"There'll be special achievement rosettes for the

team which collects the most treasures as well as a horsy prize for each member."

My heart gave a little jump. If I could win two rosettes in one day Mum and Dad would be mega-impressed.

"Are there any more questions?" Guy waited, seeming anxious to get on.

"Just one." Craig waved his arm. I looked away quickly. Ever since the Chase me Charlie he'd treated me as if I was invisible. I couldn't help feeling a sting of rejection.

"Yes, Craig?" Even Guy bristled with dislike.

"I was just wondering, Mr Marshall," he said, loitering by the window having hardly listened to a word about the treasure hunt, "Could this possibly be Cindy Morell coming up the drive in the black and gold horsebox?"

Hysteria swept through the saloon. Within seconds, everybody had forgotten the treasure hunt and dashed outside. Cindy was driving the lorry herself and we could vaguely see a horse's head through one of the six windows.

"It's mega." Sophie grabbed my arm in excitement.

Steph rushed out of the saloon with a pen and notepad. "I've got to get her autograph!"

"What's going on?" Jodie appeared at my elbow, refusing to get caught up in the euphoria.

Cindy hopped down from the cab, wearing a pair of mauve jodhpurs and leather boots with spurs. Her sunglasses covered most of her face but her mouth curled up in a smug smile. Something seemed to be amusing her.

"What's wrong with you two?" Steph came back a minute later, triumphantly waving a piece of paper with Cindy's autograph. "She's really nice." She narrowed her eyes at Jodie. "You made her out to be awful."

Suddenly a loud, piercing neigh and a clattering of hoofs made everyone flinch in alarm. Guy strode up the horsebox ramp. All the riding school horses barged against their doors, Buzby with a thatch of hay between his ears. Minstrel started rearing and snorting and Jodie had to dash over to shut his top door. As a stallion he always became more excitable than the others.

Sophie rushed over after talking to Sandra. "I've found out what's going on," she said, her face glowing with excitement. "Guy's buying a horse from Cindy and having it here on a week's trial. It's an intermediate eventer—"

Before she could finish, a huge dun horse of about seventeen hands scrabbled down the ramp, hauling Guy for a few strides before it felt the jerk of the lead rein and came back to a halt. Cindy

34

quietly observed everything from near the house where she was talking to Mrs Brentford.

The horse was fantastic. Its coat gleamed like golden syrup. It had a black mane and tail and black points which was normal for a dun horse, but around its eyes were unusual shadowy black rings. Cindy must have read everybody's thoughts because she shouted across, "Her stable name's Panda, for obvious reasons."

Guy was besotted. He couldn't stop patting or stroking her even when she gave him several friendly nips. Frank was the biggest riding school horse but he was half-Shire. Panda was big but athletic with it and really beautiful.

Annoyed that she had to stand still, she nudged Guy's shoulder, and managed to knock him slightly off balance in spite of his strength.

"So what do you think?" Guy was chuckling as he spotted us edging closer, dying to give Panda a stroke. Steph stared at him as if he'd gone crazy. Guy's brown eyes which were his best feature had softened to putty. He was hooked. "Isn't she the most fantastic girl in the world?"

"Well how was I to know he was talking about a horse?" Steph's face throbbed with annoyance at making such a gaffe. "Anybody else could have made the same mistake. I mean, the most fantastic girl in the world – it *had* to be a woman."

Rachel and Sophie howled with laughter and we clunked our crops together as we always did before the start of a lesson or a hack for good luck. I tightened Buzby's girth and felt the first drops of rain slither down my neck. Oh please let it stay fine, I thought. We all looked up at the leaden sky. The last thing we needed was to spend three hours digging up chocolate eggs and various other weird objects in the pouring rain.

Steph, Sophie and Kate were called up to the start which was at the end of the drive where Guy and Sandra were standing holding red armbands.

"Leave some treasure for us," Jodie shouted.

Minstrel whirled round in tight circles, his powerful red neck glistening like an oil slick as he lathered up in excitement. A couple of riders from the other teams shot admiring looks at Jodie as she coaxed him forward without the slightest show of nerves. Jodie had taken over the stallion when nobody else dared ride him. He belonged to Sophie but Jodie now had him on permanent loan. Sophie wasn't competitive and Rocket, who belonged to the riding school, suited her down to the ground.

Buzby shuffled forward, sulking because he had to carry the saddlebags. I dropped in line behind

Rachel and Rusty and was just about to shout to Jodie when a weird sensation shuddered right through me. It felt as if someone was staring straight through my back. Unable to stop myself, I glanced round.

And there was Craig. He was right behind me on Foxy and his eyes were like stones. He didn't smile or even move a muscle, but just stared back at me as if I didn't exist.

"What shall we do now?" Jodie cantered back up the grassy track on Minstrel who thought the last two hours had been one big hoot and was still bursting with energy. Buzby came to a dead stop as he heard me undoing the velcro fastening on my pocket. He wouldn't move forward until I'd given him three wine gums which he slurped for ages.

"We've got sixteen." Rachel crossed off the feather and the dock leaf which we'd found by the stream along with a stone which would have to pass as round and white. For the last half hour we hadn't found anything and had just ridden round and round in endless circles. Kate, Steph and Sophie were just ahead and had turned off the track in the direction of the stables. Heavy black clouds were looming.

"I think we ought to call it quits," said Rachel,

propping her knees up over the saddle flaps and resting her elbows.

Rachel and Jodie were my two closest friends, except for Sophie who was more like a big sister really. Rachel was the quietest and had only been riding for a few months. She suffered from asthma and was only allowed to ride if she had someone with her. She was already a better rider than Steph who'd been going to Brook House for three years. Rusty was her favourite pony and since she'd been at the stables he'd had a new lease of life. At twenty years old he could hold his own with any of the other ponies.

Jodie was the most practical and the best rider by far. Guy said she could be a professional if she stuck at it and Minstrel was already winning at shows. Everybody paid attention to Jodie, even Kate. Mrs Brentford said Jodie had an old head on young shoulders.

"We can't go back," I gulped, suddenly aware of what Rachel was saying. "We can't, we've got four more treasures to find."

"Emma, what is the matter with you?" Jodie looked bemused. "And why have you suddenly turned ultra-competitive – you're usually the first to give in."

"Just because winning this treasure hunt is

important to me, OK? I – I can't explain." And I couldn't – not about my parents.

"I don't want Minstrel out in a storm." Jodie was trying her best to keep the stallion calm, but he hated standing still for more than five seconds and he seemed to sense a storm was brewing.

"You go on," I said, trying to sound matter of fact. "I'll catch up – there's just one more place I want to check."

"But Guy said we weren't to split up." Rachel fiddled with her reins, concerned.

"We're not," I replied lightly. "I'll be fifteen minutes, if that, and who's going to know?"

Minstrel started pawing at the stony track and jerking his head up and down to show he was bored. "We'll come with you," said Jodie, but she sounded reluctant.

"Look, guys, will you just give me some space, please?"

Buzby strode down the narrow bridleway, convinced we must be taking a short cut, for why else would we be leaving the others? I shortened my reins to cross a wooden bridge over a dyke, then let him stretch into canter down a grassy track which ran alongside Rhododendron Wood. Mrs Brentford owned part of the wood where we had cross-country fences and where we'd be competing on the last day of pony week.

It was exhilarating to be alone for once with no instructor barking instructions and no other riders getting in the way. Buzby seemed to enjoy the freedom and I didn't have to squeeze him half as hard to keep him in canter.

On the edge of Mrs Brentford's boundary was a wooden shed which must have been used by the gamekeeper years ago. We called it Rhododendron Shed and were always dreaming of converting it into a secret headquarters for the Six Pack. I was positive I'd seen some toadstools growing round the back last Sunday when Sophie and I had come on a group hack. If we could just take back one more treasure, it might be the difference between winning and losing. I was desperate for another special achievement rosette. I could think of nothing else.

Buz slowed down abruptly and I had to grasp the martingale strap to keep my balance. A rabbit scuttled across the track, followed by a pheasant which disappeared into the undergrowth. Silence hung in the air. We entered the wood down a narrow track. The soft ground deadened the hoof beats and all we could hear was the gentle rustle of leaves as the breeze seemed to change direction and grow stronger. Buz became tense and I had to tap him down the shoulder to keep him moving forward.

There was the shed. It was just ahead, sur-
rounded by wild rhododendron bushes which had
been an expanse of dense colour earlier in the year.
Mrs Brentford had been in the local paper asking
people to preserve our national heritage and not
to leave litter on footpaths.

I jumped off and dragged Buzby forward. He
groaned until he spotted some thick, luxuriant
grass. There was no way I'd get him to go behind
the shed so I took off the lead rope wrapped round
my waist and attached it to the head collar under
his bridle. Then I unfastened the reins so he
wouldn't stand on them and tied him to a branch
in a quick release knot but with enough rope to
allow him to carry on eating.

The toadstools were in a cluster, half out of
sight, and I snapped off the largest and wrapped
it carefully in a tissue. Seventeen out of twenty.
Surely we had to win. Then I noticed that another
one of the pale peach stalks had been broken off
near the base and as I stood up, I caught sight of
the hoof marks stamped into the grass. Somebody
had already been here.

I suddenly became aware of the black, rain-
laden sky. A nervous shiver rippled up my back.
The practical voice in my head told me to stop
being so stupid, and that there was nothing to be

afraid of. But even so, I shrank back in a sudden wave of fear.

I yelled Buzby's name to break the heavy silence and it echoed through the trees as if the wood was whispering back to me. Buz shot up his head and looked at me like a naughty schoolboy and I felt all right again. Of course I wasn't all alone – I had Buz, and he was mean enough to scare anybody off. A smile forced its way onto my lips as I thought about how much he'd improved. When I first rode him he used to go down on one knee to throw riders off. He cow-kicked and bucked and deliberately trod on people's toes. For a lovely moment, I really felt, more than ever before, that he was my very own pony.

A wild thrashing from the shed cut through the silence making us both jump with terror. My heart pounded beneath my ribs. Something was banging against the window in a frenzy and I knew instinctively that it was alive. Buzby's huge brown eyes were glued to the shed, his body alert and his jaw half open, trailing uneaten grass. If it was something really bad he'd have pulled backwards by now. I forced myself to turn round and look, swallowing deeply, my stomach muscles clenching at the thought of what I might see . . .

It was a bird. A sparrow. It was flying into the window and stunning itself over and over again, desperate to escape. It must have got in through the roof.

I breathed a long sigh of relief. I'd have to open the door and free it. And quickly. Before the poor thing knocked itself out. The shed was very low, but with a sturdy bolt which seemed much too big for the door.

I hauled it back and peered into the musty dimness. There was an old chair in the corner and some kind of stove. A roll of netting was propped up in the far corner together with some wooden crates. The sparrow was perched on one of them, its beady eyes darting to the open door. Its needle-thin legs quivered and it fluttered its left wing which had a feather hanging loose.

"Poor little thing," I whispered, ducking my head as I stepped inside with the intention of shooing it out. It blinked at me once and then seeing an escape route, it launched itself upwards and hovered in the air for a few seconds, panic-stricken. I clapped my hands and it swerved through the doorway and out into the fresh air and freedom. I'd saved its life.

Suddenly a deafening crack of thunder ripped through the dark sky. I swung my head round to the window to see Buzby rooted to the spot, paralysed with fear, his eyes rolling wildly. We had to get out of here. One of the trees could fall at any minute. I felt sick with fright, and knew I'd done the wrong thing coming here. I should have listened to Jodie.

I rushed to the door, but was just a stride away when it crashed shut, cutting off most of the the light. I blinked in the sudden darkness then heard the bolt scraping against wood.

"No!" I flew forward, groping for a handle – anything. Footsteps shuffled and then the bolt slammed across with a sickening thud. Somebody had locked me in.

"No, let me out! There's someone in here! Let me out!" I was screaming at the top of my voice, fighting to be heard over the noise of the storm, but no one came back. Crazy with fear, I turned and banged my fists against the window.

Buzby twirled round and round under the trees, as trapped as I was. There, on the edge of the clearing, I caught a glimpse of somebody. Yes, whoever it was turned and hesitated, then moved away, ducking under the low branches. Their coat snagged on one of the brambles – a kind of purple mac with chevron stripes. And then nothing. Just a blur of trees and a heavy curtain of pounding rain.

My lips began to tremble. I hunched my shoulders and let my head droop, feeling suddenly weary. I pressed my forehead against the cold glass of the window, trying to work out what to do next. I'd been locked in here deliberately. Of that I was sure. And whoever had done it, was a very sick kind of person. Because there was an innocent pony at risk, not just a brainless girl who shouldn't be here in the first place.

The second crack of thunder sounded as if it were splitting the earth. My mind was numb. I was cold to the core. I felt like someone else as I stared at the terrified pony under the trees, jerking against the lead rope, struggling now in a blind panic to break free. I'd let him down. I was putting him through a nightmare. I had to do something.

Groping wildly round the shed my hands brushed one of the wooden crates. My only chance of escape was through the window which meant shattering the glass. I picked up the crate and dragged it over to the window. It was too heavy and I knew I wouldn't be able to swing it with enough force. If only there was more light.

A jagged streak of lightning dazzled the sky. It illuminated Buzby, who was cowering and drenched. His saddle had slipped to one side. At that moment I felt as if my heart had been torn apart.

I was just about to sling the crate at the window in a desperate attempt when there was another crash of thunder on the far side of the wood. I could almost feel the ground tremble. Dropping the crate I fell against the window and stared out with my hands cupped to my face. Buzby had gone. There was no sign of him. He could put a leg in a rabbit hole and injure himself! He could get lost in the woods! He could run into a car!

I had to calm down. Stay calm. Get a grip. I reached out to steady myself, fumbling against the wall, feeling a narrow shelf and something hard and cold – a hammer.

Chapter Five

The muscles in the back of my legs were burning and I felt as if my heart was going to burst, but I kept on running.

The storm had rolled away, leaving a steady downpour of rain and a greyness that matched my spirits. I'd followed Buzby's hoof marks back to the track where I'd left Jodie and Rachel but after that the rain had washed them away. He could be anywhere. Please, please let him be OK. Let him be tucked up in his stable back at Brook House. Let no one notice that we had disappeared. But I knew that was an impossible wish; they probably had search parties out right now. Guy was going to go beserk. He'd already given me a warning.

I knew I would never feel quite the same again. Something had changed inside me. I wasn't the same young girl any more. I had grown up a lot in a short space of time.

There were no cars in the stable yard and no one was around. I cut through between the barn and the manege and headed towards the office. Sophie ran out of the saloon, her face white.

"Oh thank God!" She threw her arms round me. "You're drenched," she gasped. "They're all out looking for you. Apart from Guy. He's ringing the vet."

"What?" My blood ran cold. "W-what's happened?"

Sophie shrank back, hesitating, scrabbling for a way to soften the blow. "It's Buzby, he came back. B-but he's in a bad way – he ran into some barbed wire."

"Where?" I barged towards his stable but Sophie grabbed my arm. "No, Em, he needs stitches."

"No!" My voice spiralled upwards in disbelief.

Guy hurried out of the house, his face tight with worry. "What happened? Why didn't you stay with the others?"

There were no words. No explanations. I just stared.

"The vet's on his way." Guy's voice was strained. "He needs stitches and it looks as if he's chipped a bone."

I lurched back in shock. "I must see him," I croaked.

"Just go and sit down, Emma. You've done enough damage."

"But he's my pony."

"He's a riding school pony," said Guy, walking away.

Sophie put her arm round my shoulders. "He's just upset," she reasoned, "he's got a soft spot for Buz and he's worried about losing his job. He'll be all right once the vet's been."

My knees crumpled under me and Sophie supported me towards the saloon. Once inside I thought I was going to faint. I covered my face with both hands, determined not to cry. Sophie insisted on peeling off my wet coat and the squashed toadstool fell out onto the bare floor.

I sat shivering, hugging myself with my arms. "Oh Sophie, you'll never believe what happened to me," I sobbed. And the whole bizarre nightmare came rushing out.

Just about everybody wrote messages for Buzby and pinned them up on the saloon noticeboard:

Get well soon, Buz, you're the best. Love Kate.
We love you heaps. Amy and Ben.
Thanks for always being so kind. Ebony Jane.
You're the best stablemate ever. XXX Archie.

With a shaking hand I added my message in the bottom left-hand corner.

I really love Buzby. He is one of my best friends.

I'd been frozen out by four of the girls who rode him regularly at weekends – as if I wasn't already being torn apart by guilt and remorse. Guy had grudgingly let me go to the stable once the vet had left, and I had been deeply shocked.

Buzby's head sagged down between his knees. He didn't come to the door like he usually did but stood hunched up. All down his near hind leg was a zigzag of black stitches which had been covered with antiseptic powder. He was holding it slightly askew from the hock downwards which filled me with a gloomy dread. If the X-rays showed a fracture Buz might never be able to be ridden again. At best he would be off work for months and it would cost the earth. Mrs Brentford might decide it was kinder and cheaper to have him put down.

I couldn't bear the thought. I tore myself away and locked myself in the outside toilet and cried and cried until there were no tears left.

Sophie eventually tapped on the door and hissed through the crack that there were people waiting.

"We're having a Six Pack meeting in Rocket's stable," she urged. "Please, Em, you've got to be there. We're starting in half an hour. . ." Her voice trailed off.

Sophie had believed me when I'd told her I'd been deliberately locked in Rhododendron Shed, but would the others? Of course they wouldn't.

They'd say I was exaggerating as usual. I stood up and groped around for another toilet roll to use to blow my nose.

It was only then that I noticed the supermarket carrier bag pushed out of sight behind the toilet pipes. Immediately I thought it must belong to one of the riding school pupils – kids often came straight from school and got changed for their evening lessons. I'd give it to Sandra and she could put a notice on the lost-and-found board.

I grabbed the bag and gasped in horror when I saw what was inside. I couldn't believe it. With trembling hands I pulled the wet garment away from the clinging plastic. Just the touch of the material made my skin crawl. It was a purple coat with very definite chevron stripes.

Whoever had locked me in the shed had realized they'd been seen and quickly hidden their coat behind the toilet pipes. It was frightening to think that it could be anyone at the stables.

"Oh come on, you know what Emma's like for exaggerating – it'll be another one of her fantasies." Steph's spiteful high-pitched voice floated over Rocket's stable door, but somehow it didn't really register. I was walking in a daze, clutching the plastic bag under my own riding mac. The wonderful, friendly riding school had suddenly become an ominous place. Just a moment earlier I'd bumped into Sandra shaking up a fresh straw bed in Panda's stable and complaining about Guy being more interested in showjumping and Cindy Morell than in the riding school ponies. We'd suspected for ages that Sandra suspected was secretly in love with him. Nobody seemed straightforward any more. I left her coughing and spluttering as she forked up the straw banks moaning about the dust and spores.

Everybody on pony week had gone home for the evening. It was past five o'clock. The winners of the treasure hunt had collected eighteen items – we wouldn't have won anyway. There was no sign of Craig.

I walked into the stable feeling like a zombie. "We were just talking about what happened," explained Sophie, "about what you told me."

There was an awkward pause. My five friends shuffled uneasily, full of doubt. Kate was the first to speak. "Are you sure you didn't imagine it, Em? I mean, it's a pretty nasty thing to do."

I waited for a moment, then dug into the bag and pulled out the coat. Kate's mouth fell open. Rocket swivelled round, stretching his lead rope, sensing the tension. I told them where I'd found it and what this must mean.

52

"But – but who'd want to do that?" Jodie's face crinkled into an expression of disgust.

"The only person I've been able to think of is Craig." I leant against the stable wall drained of energy.

"But you've been so nice to him," said Rachel.

"You didn't see his face after I'd beaten him in the Chase me Charlie." I could still picture Craig's cold eyes and knew he was capable of anything.

"Look, all we have to do is prove who this coat belongs to," said Kate. She picked it up and busily examined the pockets and lining, but I'd already checked it for a name-tape.

"Never mind that, let's go straight to Guy." Sophie was already marching for the door.

"No way." I said firmly. "He won't believe me, he'll think we've made it all up. I'll just be in worse trouble."

"So what do we do? Let *you* take all the blame?" Sophie was really rattled.

"Wait till he cracks," said Jodie, levering herself up from where she was sitting in the straw. "He'll see that the coat has gone from his hiding place and it'll unnerve him. If he's got an ounce of decency in him, he'll own up."

"We'll be waiting till hell freezes over," Steph stated flatly.

"Oh, I nearly forgot," cried Rachel, her hand

flying to her mouth. "I heard the girl with the plaits talking earlier – Craig was playing the dunce at first because he wants to win the Most Improved Rider Trophy. He's quite experienced really."

"Hence the sudden improvement in the jumping," Kate snarled. "God, Em, you certainly know how to pick 'em. He really is the ultimate nightmare pen pal."

We all joined hands and agreed to say nothing, at least for the moment. "You may regret it," warned Sophie as we filed out of the stable. I glanced across to the office and saw Guy deep in conversation with both my parents.

"I can't for the life of me understand why you left that pony tied up." Mum was in the passenger seat going on and on. Dad was hunched over the driving wheel, staring straight ahead.

"This is my point, Wendy, there's not enough discipline at that riding school, they're allowed to run wild. There'll be an accident, mark my words, and it won't just be one of the ponies."

I glared out of the window, not bothering to explain that Buzby's future was hanging in the balance.

"This is why she'd be so much better off doing another sport – hockey for instance – and she'd meet some nice people." Mum and Dad had never actually said it but they looked down their noses at Steph, Kate and Rachel for not living in good areas. Mum and Dad were terrible snobs.

The houses rolled past, one after another, all neat and tidy as we turned into our avenue. I didn't want to play hockey. I wanted to keep going to Brook House where people lived life to the full, where jeans were acceptable and horses were everything. I wanted to become a riding instructor one day and live in a cottage with a paddock and stables.

I ran up the stairs to my bedroom and slammed the door. It was painted lilac with horse pictures all over one wall. I'd wanted purple, and lilac had been a compromise. Mickey, my hamster, was running like mad on his wheel. He always woke up at four o'clock when I came in from school. He shot inside a toilet roll tube and peered out from the other side.

Mum came in with a mug of tea and a pile of biscuits an hour later. "Listen, don't take too much notice of your dad," she said smiling. "You know he's all bark. He just worries about something happening to you – he can't help it. He thinks another sport would be less dangerous."

"Less expensive," I forced out through gritted teeth.

"Now Emma, that's not fair, we've always done our best for you."

"Yeah, sorry . . ." I hesitated. "But Mum, I'm growing up, I'm not six any more. I should be able to make my own choices."

"I know." She held my hand and I squeezed hers hard, watching her eyes soften with affection and crease at the corners. "But you'll always be our little baby."

I drank the tea and threw the biscuits out of the window. I didn't know what else to do with them. Two blackbirds pecked at them viciously until a crow swooped down from next door's roof and scared them off.

I pulled my "Milton" duvet over my legs, opened up *Horses from A to Z: The Manual* and started reading. It was the only thing that would take my mind off Buzby.

I knew it was a nightmare before I'd even opened my eyes but I still sat up with a start, my breath tight in my chest. Light was streaming through the curtains but when I fumbled for the alarm clock it only said 4.30 a.m. It was still the middle of the night.

I'd dreamt that Buzby was going to be put down and Guy and the vet were huddled in a corner, talking about injections and humane methods of killing. Everybody at the riding school was blaming me, whispering "Murderer, murderer." I flung back the duvet and sat with my head between my knees, recovering. On the far wall was a colour picture of Buzby with a rosette for clear round jumping at the Horseworld Show. He looked so happy and healthy. I knew I couldn't stay in bed a moment longer. I had to see him.

I pulled on an old grey tracksuit and trainers and reached for the door handle. I crept slowly down the stairs and slipped out of the back door. The air was sharp with a freshness only possible in the early hours.

It was three miles to the stables and I planned to take my mountain bike. The spare key to the garage winked cheerfully at me from underneath the mat where we kept it. Mum was always saying we shouldn't keep it in such an obvious place. There was the bike, all ready and waiting. Not long now, Buzby. With a sudden feeling of dread I realized it was only four hours before Guy would be ringing the vet to discover the results of the X-ray.

The stable yard was shrouded in a hazy grey light and the dawn chorus was in full swing as I gently slipped off my bike and pushed it up the drive. Quarter to six. It seemed to have taken for ever. I realized I'd be in trouble later, but when I saw Buzby's stable, tucked away behind the saloon, I knew I couldn't have done anything else.

He was standing at the back when I peered in. He lifted his head and blinked a few times and then tried to move forward but changed his mind. I welled up again. Buzby always dashed to his door – he always knew there would be a special titbit on offer.

The stitches were still in place, clotted with congealed blood here and there. Bits of straw clung to the hairs and I spent ages trying to pick them off, delicately catching them between my fingernails and tweaking them out. It was all my fault. How could I even think about having a pony of my own? I wasn't responsible. I wasn't even a good rider.

A racking cough from the next-door stable brought me back to reality. A horse was coughing badly. It didn't seem to be able to get its breath. It was Panda, of course – Cindy Morell's gorgeous dun mare. I remembered Sandra making up a straw bed for her and saying they were moving her into that stable because it was the biggest in the yard.

I hurried from one stable to the next. What if she had something stuck in her throat? What if she was choking? She was standing with her head slung low, her eyes unfocused and glazed and her jaw half open, waiting for the next heaving spasm.

I didn't have a clue what to do. She hardly noticed me as I rushed to her shoulder. Her flanks and stomach muscles were tensed and clenched into knots.

"Panda, what is it, what's wrong?" She stared at me, her eyes full of fear, then tried to stagger forward as if to escape the pain. I had to get help. I had to go to the house.

Whirling round, I fled out and across the yard towards the rickety garden gate and the cottage where Mrs Brentford would be tucked up in bed. It was twenty past six. Old people weren't supposed to sleep that well. Maybe she was already up?

I banged urgently on the front door. Then I noticed the doorbell and kept my finger on it. Where was she? I was making enough noise to raise the dead.

"Mrs Brentford!" I yelled up at the top window, which was half-covered in creeping ivy. Suddenly a bolt rattled on the inside of the door. She was here! She was here! The door creaked open a few inches.

"Mrs Brentford, it's Emma Parker."

She fiddled for ages with the safety chain and then appeared, still in her dressing gown, looking wide-eyed with alarm. "It's Panda," I shrieked, "Guy's new horse – I think she's choking." The words tumbled out.

Mrs Brentford was sixty-nine and no bigger than me. She'd been running the riding school for years, long before Guy arrived or Sophie's dad bought in as a business partner. She'd put horses first all her life and I really admired her.

She took the catch off the door and we hurried back across the yard, not daring to speak, imagining the worst. I knew from watching *Animal Kingdom* every week that animals could very quickly choke to death.

The silence from the stable filled me with an icy dread. What if something terrible had happened? What if she was lying lifeless in the straw? Mrs Brentford took charge and pulled open the door. I forced myself to look. I didn't want to scream, I must not scream.

Panda was standing tugging gently at her hay net. She swung her head round to look at us, unperturbed.

"But, but . . ." I couldn't believe it. There was no sign whatsoever that she'd been ill. I rushed forward, running my hand down her huge neck and shoulder, desperate to find any trace of the atttack. But she wasn't even warm. Her breathing was regular and normal.

Mrs Brentford's face had tightened with annoyance. She looked ridiculous standing in a stable in her nightwear "I think we'd better go back to the house and you can tell me exactly what you're doing in my stable yard by yourself at six o'clock in the morning."

But my brain was racing along a million different channels. Something was wrong. Panda had been gasping for breath. She couldn't recover so quickly. Something had to be wrong. I knew Mrs Brentford checked all the Brook House horses last thing at night . . .

"Supposing," I blurted out, desperate for an answer, "supposing a horse was coughing in the middle of the night, would you hear them?"

Mrs Brentford turned round and stared at me. "Don't be silly, girl, I'm partially deaf," she said flatly, as if it was common knowledge.

Chapter Six

"Can you put me straight through to Mr Nielsen?" Guy turned his back to me so I couldn't see his expression. "Yes, it is important."

Sophie and Rachel were in the office, sitting on either side of me. Guy was ringing the vet for Buzby's results. I felt sick with fear. The thought of Saturdays and holidays without Buzby threw me into despair. I wouldn't be able to cope.

"Don't worry, Em," said Sophie, "if it is the worst, we'll raise money, we'll do whatever it takes to make him better."

"Yeah, sponsored swims, silences, anything," said Rachel, nodding in agreement.

"I see." Guy's voice was cold and unreadable.

"I can't face it," I gulped, leaping up. I rushed out of the office and made for Buzby's stable. I wanted to run my hands through his mane one more time as if everything was normal. What would Mrs Brentford do with him? He wouldn't be any good for anything. We'd be a matching pair.

I heard Guy's footsteps behind me.

"I don't want to hear," I said in a hard, bright voice that wasn't mine.

"Oh. Not even if it's good news?"

I turned round ever so slowly, to see the gently teasing expression in Guy's soft brown eyes. "He hasn't damaged any bones," he said grinning. "He's torn a muscle. He's going to be fine."

I was speechless.

"I'll leave you to yourself." Guy hesitated and then turned and walked back to the office. I buried my face in Buzby's thick spongy coat and cried tears of relief.

"You don't do it like that, you do it like this." Kate, in her usual bossy fashion was showing Rachel how to apply a tail bandage.

"There's no need anyway because Rusty doesn't rub his tail."

"Excuse me," said Kate raising her eyebrows, "but it's supposed to be to flatten down the hairs – you know, make him look presentable."

Rachel stared pointedly at Archie's tail which was sticking up like a toilet brush.

"Well I didn't say it worked for all ponies, did I?"

We were sitting on the grass near the saloon talking horses and generally mucking about. It was our official lunch break and Sophie was swinging her riding crop, pretending to play polo.

"You look so uncool," said Steph, wincing as Sophie sent a tennis ball hurtling across the grass.

"I don't care," she said. "If I don't practise I might hit Rocket's legs."

At two o'clock Guy was giving everyone a polo lesson with proper mallets and balls borrowed from the Pony Club. Sophie was insisting that I share Rocket with her for the rest of the week, but I didn't mind not riding. I was just so grateful that Buz was OK. I proudly held up the massive daisy chain I was making for him which would probably be devoured in thirty seconds.

Mrs Brentford had amazed me by driving me home at seven o'clock in the morning and dropping me off at the end of our avenue. All she'd said during the whole journey was that she'd once run away for three days with a Welsh mountain pony that her parents had wanted to sell. She said it was up to me whether I told my parents – it was our secret, but in her opinion the truth was better out than in. Jodie had always said that Mrs B was a really special lady and now I could see why.

Overwhelmed with gratitude, I got out of the car and ran down the pavement vowing I wouldn't sneak out in the middle of the night again. When Dad came shuffling to the door, dazed with sleep,

I bottled out and made up a bizarre story that I'd been sleepwalking and had locked myself out. Sometimes the truth is just too hard to tell.

"Crikey, Em, that's the first time I've seen you nibble the chocolate off a Mars Bar instead of devouring it whole". Steph's voice interrupted my thoughts and I quickly put the chocolate back in its wrapper and slung it into my bag.

"What's up with you? Has your stomach suddenly shrunk?" said Steph bitting into a crisp. She didn't miss a thing.

I'd been watching Panda out in the paddock, playfully nudging the besotted Frank, then turning and clipping up her heels, swirling round and cantering off. She didn't have anything wrong with her now, in fact she was a picture of health. I couldn't mention the coughing attack to Guy because I'd then have to explain why I'd been in her stable in the early hours of the morning. Mrs Brentford quite clearly thought there was nothing seriously wrong. So why couldn't I just forget it?

"It's ridiculous," said Sandra, tightening up Ebony Jane's girth, "she's only hiring her for hacks yet she's insisted on changing her diet, and her tack. Next she'll be wanting her in a side-saddle or something equally stupid."

Cindy Morell was not one of Sandra's favourite people, especially since lunchtime when she'd rung twice to say she'd like the mare in a different bit if possible. Poor Ebby looked uncomfortable with the new jointed snaffle and flash noseband. "You know what an angel she is," said Sandra as she brushed the straw out of Ebby's tail. "You could ride her in a head collar and she'd still be as good as gold."

I reached up and stroked the bay mare's pretty forehead with the zigzaggy star slightly off centre. I wouldn't want Cindy Morell on my back at any cost.

"Of course Guy is so taken up with Panda he'll say yes to anything. Do you know that he's even taking out a bank loan to pay for her? He must be out of his tree."

I knew Sandra shouldn't be gossiping about her boss like this but I couldn't help worrying about Ebby. Sandra did a good job at looking after all the horses although sometimes she'd cut corners and we'd hear Guy asking her to do something again.

"Anyway," she went on, looking up and rubbing at her freckled nose, "when are you going to wise up and tell Guy what really happened in Rhododendron Wood and drop that cocky, jumped-up, so-called friend of yours in at the deep end?"

66

I stiffened in alarm and then dropped my eyes as Sandra continued to stare straight at me. "How did you know about that?" I gulped.

Sandra tossed her dyed bobbed hair. "Walls have ears you know," she said. "And grooms are a bit like waiters. People carry on talking and forget they're there."

"The whole idea of polo is to hit the ball and keep it moving." Guy surprised us by jumping onto Archie to give a demonstration. The wily Palomino was goggle-eyed and for the first time in his life behaved impeccably.

"I never knew he could move so fast," said Rachel, shielding her eyes with her hand.

"It doesn't say much for your riding, Kate," Steph giggled. "You turn beetroot just getting him to trot."

"Ssssh." Two girls on our right who were taking it mega-seriously scowled at us.

"Are you sure you don't want a ride, Em?" Sophie swivelled Rocket round to face me.

"The assets of a good polo player are an eye for the ball, physical strength, courage, fitness and mental alertness," Guy boomed out.

"Does that answer your question?" I glanced up at Sophie who was fiddling with one of her knee-pads. Rocket took the opportunity to sneeze all over me. I was secretly glad that I'd missed the polo training because the last time someone had tried to teach me eye-ball contact I'd accidentally hit them with the racket.

I clasped my arms over my chest and looked at my feet, suddenly aware that Craig was staring at me from the other side of the circle.

"The best ponies for polo are usually gymkhana ponies so, Rachel and Sophie, we'll have you out first. Now you must stand up in the stirrups to hit the ball and lean towards it." Guy gave a demonstration and smacked the ball down the field where it bounced off a tree.

Steph was busy picking at her chipped nail varnish and didn't notice Monty nibbling at her mallet.

"Excellent!" shouted Rachel, weaving Rusty after the ball and doing a fantastic job of neck-reining.

"I think I ought to call it quits now." Jodie started circling Minstrel. "Have you ever seen an Arab stallion doing a polo tackle?" She sounded worried.

"You mean riding someone off," I corrected vaguely, feeling increasingly uncomfortable.

When I next looked up, Craig was riding towards me on Foxy.

"Is it OK if I change my helmet?" he asked,

already tipping it off his head as I stared down at the pile of equipment around me. Guy had called everyone into a line to practise strokes and I felt alarmingly alone.

"I'm really pleased that Buzby's going to be all right."

"I bet you are," I snapped, thrashing around for another hat to pass to him.

"No, really I am. It would have been terrible if . . ."

"What? If he'd have had to be put down?" I glared at him.

Craig's voice came stiffly through his pale lips. "I hoped we might be friends."

"Oh please. Is that all you wanted to tell me? Isn't there something else you want to get off your chest – a confession perhaps?"

For the first time there was a crack in his coolness. His eyes hardened to a cold watchfulness. "I don't think so." His lips had gone very pale.

"You'd better get back to the group." Even as I said it I realized I was letting him off the hook. "Let me know if anyone's lost a coat," I shouted to his departing back, but he didn't turn round.

Ebony Jane's stable stood empty. Somehow I wasn't in the mood for polo any more so I'd decided to go back and check on Buzby.

Sandra was sitting in the sunniest spot in the yard, supposedly cleaning tack but going to great lengths to catch the sun on her legs.

"Her Majesty left about an hour ago to go on a hack," she volunteered, splashing lotion on her freckly arms. "Anyone would think I was her lady-in-waiting the way she had me running around."

I could visualize Ebby's steady walk and Cindy nudging her on, demanding more and more from her.

"I'll be in Buzby's stable if anyone wants me," I said.

Buzby was confined to box-rest for a whole month and he was already throwing the water bucket round the stable in boredom.

"Now you've just got to put up with it," I told him, tapping his nose, and then felt guilty for reprimanding him. He immediately nuzzled my jeans pocket and sniffed out a boiled sweet.

Why had pony week turned into such a huge disaster? A heaviness kept dragging at my spirits despite the joy of knowing Buzby was all right. Lack of sleep had stretched my nerves to breaking point. Why was it that the things we looked forward to the most, often didn't live up to our expectations? I vowed to expect little from life in the future; then anything good would be a pleasant surprise.

70

Buzby started to chew my hair as a subtle indication that he was passing out with hunger.

"OK, you win." I jumped up, grabbing hold of the empty water bucket. "I'll find you a gourmet meal which will shut you up, at least until the vet arrives."

The verges on either side of the front drive were tropical paradises of lush grass. Buzby would truly be in heaven once he got his nose lodged in the bucket. Juicy green stains spread across my hands as I methodically snatched clump after clump of grass and pressed them down.

From the age of three my ears had been trained to pick up horses' hoofs like radar, so it was no surprise that I heard Ebby before she was even in sight. I jerked upright and waited tensely for her to round the corner.

She appeared on the grass verge trotting forward stiffly, Cindy's powerful seat driving her on. I was about to step forward to go and meet them when something happened which made me stop in my tracks.

For no apparent reason, Cindy raised her arm and her whip cut through the air and cracked into Ebby's quarters.

Chapter Seven

"Why didn't you tell someone?" Sophie sat next to me on a straw bale, quietly listening as I poured out the whole story.

"I'm in enough trouble as it is," I explained. "Nobody's going to take my side against Cindy Morell." Even Sophie didn't disagree. I'd told her about my secret trip to the stables and Panda's mystery cough and then, most importantly about Ebony Jane.

"This is Six Pack business," Sophie said solemnly. "Anything that involves the welfare of the riding school horses means we have to stand united. I'll call a meeting straight away."

"Do you think they'll believe me?"

"Oh Em, do you really have to ask?" And of course I didn't. On anything really serious my friends had never let me down.

"But I think now we'd better go and watch Guy showjumping Panda. It's the first time she's been exercised since the coughing attack. We may pick up some vital clue."

Guy was trying Panda out on the arena over some really high showjumps. The polo training had finished and everybody had been told to groom their ponies and clean their tack before they went home.

But everybody apart from Craig was glued to the arena watching Cindy put up the jumps and the beautiful dun mare soar over them. Rachel and Jodie had drawn the short straws and were staying in the stable yard to keep an eye on Craig in case he was getting up to some mischief.

"She looks fantastic." Steph moved a seat closer to get a better look. "How high do you think she can jump?"

"Six foot at least," Sophie answered. "That spread over there must be five foot three and she's making nothing of it." Guy was such a good rider that Panda took off at exactly the right spot every time. We were too inexperienced to do that but since Guy had explained about keeping our legs on and sitting still until the very last stride we'd all improved enormously.

Panda's black ears cocked forward as she bunched for the upright which Cindy had raised. "I told you she was good," she said. Her clipped voice made my skin crawl after what I'd seen her do to Ebby.

Panda had been a successful event horse doing

dressage and cross-country as well, but she was so good at jumping that Cindy had decided to sell her as a showjumper.

"She looks fine so far." Sophie was watching Panda like a hawk. There was no sign of a cough. I didn't know whether to be relieved or disappointed.

"I think that's enough for today." Cindy's voice suddenly took on a hard edge.

Guy circled Panda and pulled to a halt obviously wanting to do more but not arguing. "I definitely want her," he said grinning, "she's sensational."

"A world beater." Cindy patted the golden, muscle-packed neck. "I wasn't exaggerating, was I?"

Guy disappeared under the saddle flap to loosen the girth and a triumphant smile flickered over Cindy's face. "Perhaps you could write out the cheque over dinner?"

"A waste of time." Jodie came out of the saloon with Rachel, struggling with a pile of clean tack. "Craig hasn't put a foot out of place, he's got no intentions of owning up, Emma. You've got to tell Guy about Rhodedendron Shed before it's too late, before he tries something else."

"I don't think he'll be trying any more stunts," said Kate, running up, breathless and excited. "I've just seen him leaving the toilet, obviously going back for the coat. He was as white as a sheet – he knows he's been sprung."

The vet arrived soon after Guy had finished riding Panda and both Guy and Cindy went with him into Buzby's stable. It was only supposed to be a routine check-up but they'd been in there for ages. I could see their dark outlines moving around through the stable window.

Just about everybody had gone home apart from Kate and Steph who were doing a horsy jigsaw in the saloon, killing time waiting for Kate's mum. Everyone was meeting in town at the ice rink at seven for the pony week social outing. Kate's mum had organized it together with a couple of the other mothers and Guy. They'd even laid on a special minibus. The Six Pack would have rather gone to a horsy demonstration but had been outvoted.

I picked up the yard brush and absent-mindedly swept two blades of straw back and forth. I couldn't stand not knowing what was going on. Somebody put a hand over Buzby's door to pull back the bolt and then hesitated and carried on talking.

I felt as if I was going to scream. Then I noticed a trickle of water spreading from under Panda's door. She'd knocked over her water bucket . . . And her stable was right next to Buz's. It was the perfect excuse to get closer.

"Of course in my opinion the Conservative government brought about their own downfall. Now when I get elected as councillor . . ."

I couldn't believe it. They weren't talking about Buzby at all. They were talking about politics. I was crouched inside Panda's stable listening at the wooden divide. Guy was making every attempt to escape but Mr Nielsen was obviously on his favourite subject.

"Well at least Buzby is making a full recovery," Guy butted in.

I closed my eyes and felt the warm relief surge through me. Buzby was OK. I shuffled slightly as I felt pins and needles in my left leg. My concentration settled on Panda who oddly hadn't come across to snuffle my hair and look for titbits as every horse usually did. Sandra had forgotten to put on her cooler rug. My eyes drifted over her strong shoulders and deep girth to her powerful quarters and then back to her flanks. She was standing near her hay net but not eating. Was it my imagination or was she . . .? I studied her ribcage more closely. It was rising up and down in a rhythm but every time she drew in air there seemed to be a double movement, like a double breath. I could see it clearly – there was something wrong. I stood up quickly and banged my head on the manger.

There was a silence from next door. I had to take the bull by the horns. I had to go and face them.

"I think there's something wrong with Panda," I blurted out.

Cindy Morell glared at me as if I was a worm crawling about on the floor. Mr Nielsen took a step forward but she shot out her hand and snatched his arm. "Don't listen to her, she keeps making things up. She even said I was being cruel to one of the riding school horses."

I gaped in shock, completely thrown. I'd only told Sophie about Ebby. She was obviously convinced I'd tell and had decided to beat me to it and discredit me.

Guy looked puzzled and then reddened with growing embarrassment. He walked foward and glanced over Panda's door, then broke into a relieved smile. "She's just got a chill – that stupid groom's left her rug off."

"There you are then." Cindy manoeuvred Mr Nielsen right away from the stable. "Nothing to worry about."

"Well I suppose I'd better get onto my next

call . . ." He hesitated for a brief moment then picked up his bag.

"What's got into you lately?" Guy hissed a few moments later. "All these fantasies of yours, Emma, are just not on. This is a riding school, not a setting for a novel. Get your feet back on the ground before I completely lose my patience."

My eyes filled up and I gulped back a sob. "Guy Marshall, I hate you," I mumbled to his departing back. Panda pushed her nose against my shoulder as if to thank me for trying. "What is it, Panda?" I stroked her kitten-soft nose. "What's wrong with you?"

The car park at the ice rink was packed so Sophie's dad pulled his Jaguar right up to the main doors. Half the Six Pack had travelled together which had been a nightmare in a way because Sophie had telephoned everyone earlier to tell them about Ebony Jane and Panda but we couldn't under any circumstances discuss it in front of her dad.

Steph irritated everyone by playing the same Spice Girls song over and over on the CD player until Sophie threatened to strangle her with the seat belt.

We spotted the minibus parked over by the fence. Kate's mum and a troop of other mums were harassing Guy as to whose daughter was the best rider. Rachel rolled her eyes and we smothered giggles as we dived through the rotating doors. It was the first time I'd laughed in ages.

Jodie and Kate were already putting on their skates and had ordered ours.

"Listen," I said, feeling really lighthearted, "let's forget about riding school business tonight and concentrate on having a really good time. What do you say?"

"Count me in," agreed Rachel collecting everybody's coats. "Let's skate till we drop."

"Er, who invited her?" Steph made a face as Cindy Morell stalked in through the doors in front of Guy. I noticed Craig was directly behind them with his head slung low, avoiding eye contact.

"It doesn't matter." I forced out the words. "We'll just ignore her. We're not going to let her ruin our night."

Sophie was the best skater, followed by Steph and then me. I was thrilled that my new pair of boot-cut trousers which I'd had for my birthday were actually loose around the waist.

Steph suggested we all link hands which we did for a while, then Kate had the idea of pretending we were doing dressage tests on ice which was hilarious, especially as we got Guy to do the judging. Sophie did the best centre line and I did the best ten metre circle.

Rachel swished across and nudged my arm, discreetly pointing to where Cindy was trying out a pair of skates and clinging onto the boards, glowering like a bull.

"I dare you to go and annoy her," she said grinning. "Go on, it'll get right up her nose."

I skated past Cindy keeping my chin in the air and my eyes fixed firmly ahead. I could feel her seething. Funnily enough it gave me a wonderful feeling of exhilaration. Turning round, I set off back, moving in even closer so I'd blast past her feeble efforts.

She grabbed my arm and before I even realized, I felt myself being hauled round and saw the boards crashing towards me. I stuck out my hand to save myself and my knuckles crunched painfully as the weight of my body slammed into the boards. Pain soared up my arm.

"Don't think I don't know what you're up to," Cindy hissed. "Don't meddle in things you know nothing about, OK?" She was so close my nostrils were twitching from the smell of her nauseating perfume.

"Leave her alone for God's sake, Banny." I jumped back, startled by Craig's voice. He was pushing her away, his face burning with anger. But he'd called her Banny. My mind struggled through the fog searching for the relevance. I'd read a personality profile once ... Yes, that was the nickname her family called her ... Family.

"Yeah you've sussed it," said Craig looking straight into my eyes, his mouth settling into a resigned smile, "Cindy is my cousin."

Chapter Eight

The quiz started first thing the next morning which left no time for us to have a proper Six Pack meeting.

Steph had brought along her plastic model of a Haflinger pony which she swore brought good luck and Rachel had spotted an Eddie Stobart lorry on her way to the riding school which she insisted was a good sign. Jodie said we were a superstitious lot and refused to have five lucky mascots on our table. We'd called ourselves the Equine Warriors and were determined to do the best we possibly could. When someone answered three questions wrong they got knocked out so that eventually there would be just one winner left, who would pick up the special achievement points and rosette. I tried to visualize the pages of *Horses from A to Z*, but only got as far as section C.

"If everybody's ready we'll begin." Guy rustled his thick pile of papers. "When is a Thoroughbred's official birthday? . . . What was the name of the first mare to win the Hickstead Derby? . . . Which brush should be used on a pony's mane and tail?"

I'd shoved my hand up in time for question two and got it right. Bluebird.

"Most greys are born black or brown. True or false? . . . A Falabella is the smallest breed of horse. True or false? . . . What is a gag?"

Most people were too keen to stick up their hand and were eliminating themselves with the wrong answers.

"How would you describe a Trakehner? . . . All ponies should be fed immediately before being ridden. True or false? . . . The poll is to be found on which part of the horse's body?"

My brain was leaping around with excitement. I knew most of the answers. It was almost as if I had so much on my mind worrying about Buzby and Panda and Ebony Jane, not to mention my parents and Cindy and Craig, that I was functioning on automatic pilot. I didn't have any nerves fizzing around and clogging up my head. Steph was studying me with muted surprise. I wasn't Emma Parker, thick and hopeless any more. I was carrying our team. I'd got five questions right.

Sophie groaned as Rachel and Steph got knocked out in quick succession. People were falling like flies now. In fact there was a reluctance to put up hands. The questions were getting harder.

"What are the symptoms of strangles?" Jodie flew up her left arm and then clapped her hand over her mouth. She gave the wrong answer and got knocked out. We were down to just Kate, Sophie and me.

"A Palomino is recognized as a breed in America, but elsewhere is only classed as a colour. True or false? . . . How many inches in a hand? . . . What is a skewbald? . . . Is ragwort a poisonous plant?"

The questions were getting easier again. Craig fired off three out of four of the answers. I was still hanging on. Then Sophie was knocked out too. There was only a handful of people left in. Craig was at the opposite side of the room concentrating like mad. I couldn't look at him or he'd put me off.

"Which side should you plait up a horse's mane? . . . Which side should you lead a pony from? . . . What is laminitis caused by?"

"Goodness, Emma, it's just you and Craig left in!" Sophie was so excited she was shouting at the top of her voice. I must stay calm. I musn't blow it. I fixed my eyes on Guy and waited for the next question.

"A pony who rubs his mane and tail raw in late spring and early summer could be suffering from what disease?"

"Sweet itch!" I shot out the answer as soon as Guy had finished the sentence.

Guy nodded and moved onto the next. "Removing droppings from a pony's field helps to control what?"

"Worms!" Craig beat me to it by seconds.

The tension was becoming unbearable. Everybody was so quiet you could hear a fly land never mind a pin drop. My mouth had turned desert-dry. For the next five minutes Craig and I shouted out answers, one after the other. It was a dead heat.

"This is no good." Guy looked flustered. "I'm going to give you each a pen and paper and you're to write down the answer to a very difficult question. There's to be no help whatsoever from your team members."

He passed us a single sheet of notepaper and I picked up the black biro which slipped through my sweaty fingers. Craig looked as if he were about to run the one hundred metres.

"Is there such a thing as a bog pony and if so where does it originate?"

I'd seen something on telly about this. Ancient bog ponies were thought to be extinct but a stallion had been found and now they were breeding them. They were called bog ponies because of their ability to pick their way through the Irish bogs. My hand scrawled the answer at a delirious speed.

Sophie passed the folded pieces of paper to Guy and we waited for the result. The Six Pack had crossed their fingers and legs and Steph was even trying to cross her eyes.

"The winner is . . ." Guy hesitated with a look of amazement. "Emma Parker."

The Six Pack went absolutely crackers. We'd won. I'd won. I pinched myself and the dream still didn't go away. Guy was walking towards me with an orange rosette. I saw Craig disappear out of the louvred doors looking tired with disappointment. I should be glad that he'd lost but I felt nothing one way or the other. All I knew was that something wonderful had happened. And for the first time in a long time I was starting to like myself again.

"I want to apologize." Craig leaned over the stable door where I was grooming Buzby. He'd got thousands of hay seeds in his mane where he'd been rubbing against his hay net. I tapped the curry comb against the wall and started again.

"Emma, are you listening?"

I shrugged and kept up the regular sweeping strokes. Buzby closed his eyes and leaned into the brush. "What are you sorry for?" I asked simply. "For being a rude pig? For lying about your riding?

Or for lying about your famous relative? Or let me think, maybe there's something else?"

"OK, you've made your point, but you know what for. I never meant it to go that far. I was just messing about."

"With other people's lives?" I stared straight ahead at Buzby's rounded withers. "Is that it with you, Craig? Is everything just a lark, regardless of the consequences?" My voice was low and almost toneless now.

"I'm going to Guy and I'm going to tell him everything." He made a sweeping gesture with his arms as if he was doing me a big favour.

"Well don't expect a medal. It's taken you long enough." I glared at his carrot-red hair and snubby nose almost with revulsion. "If all pen pals were like you, Craig, the Post Office would be out of business."

"Look," he said, clenching his fists and taking in a sharp breath, "I admit, I was wrong, I was angry that I lost the jumping and I shouldn't have locked you in that shed. But I can't change what's done. I can only attempt to fix it."

I stared at him with cool appraising eyes. "If you really want to fix things, you'll tell me what's wrong with your cousin's horse."

His face suddenly went rigid. "You've got it wrong," he said, obviously flustered. "There is

87

nothing wrong with Panda. Do you honestly think Guy would be considering buying her if there was?"

"I don't know . . ." I hesitated, my mind racing back over the events of the last few days.

"Well if you're so right," he snapped, "why has she got an up-to-date veterinary certificate saying she's in perfect health? Answer me that."

But I couldn't. My mind was blank. Any thoughts on Panda had suddenly dried up.

Sandra was mucking out Ebony Jane's stable swinging in time to her walkman. A cold feeling of dread skittered through me. Ebby wasn't there. We'd devised a plan where Jodie and Minstrel would be ready to follow Cindy as soon as she came to the stable, to try and catch her out.

I pushed mindlessly passed Craig and ran across the yard. Two hens squawked from under the wheelbarrow but Sandra still didn't hear me.

"Sandra!" I lifted up one of her earphones and yelled at her. She dropped the pitchfork in fright. "Where's Ebby?" I said lowering my voice, my face tight with worry.

"Cindy's taken her," she said. "She came when you were all doing the quiz. She's been gone ages."

"Have you any idea where she's gone?"

She shrugged her shoulders. "Haven't got a clue."

*

"This is the worst," said Steph. "Poor darling Ebby, she could be anywhere by now."

I blinked hard to shut out the picture of Cindy cracking her whip down Ebony's side. "It's my fault," I whimpered. "I should have said more – told Mrs Brentford. I shouldn't have been frightened to upset Guy. Horses should always come first."

"We'd better tell the others," Steph smoothed down her hair which immediately sprang back up again.

We found everyone except Sophie in Minstrel's stable with Jodie tightening his girth and Rachel brushing his silken tail with the body brush. Minstrel was so highly bred that he still came in at nights because otherwise he got a chill. He pushed his wonderful dished face against my coat sniffing out horse nuts.

"There's nothing we can do now," said Jodie when I told her what had happened.

"If that woman hurts one hair on Ebby's body . . ." Steph stopped, unable to finish her sentence.

"I know." Jodie kept her voice level and looked at her. "But we can't do anything until she gets back."

"Emma, I've got some fantastic news." Suddenly Sophie thundered towards me, not slowing down, her breath rasping in her throat. "Craig's told Guy what happened. In fact Guy's looking for you right now . . . But that's not the best bit. You're in line to win the Most Improved Rider trophy. Guy said so. You're the only person to win two special achievement rosettes. So . . ." She broke off and steadied her breath, the colour in her face calming down. "There's something I want you to do. I want to stand down. I want you to ride Rocket in the cross-country."

Chapter Nine

"I can't do it, I can't. Rocket's 14.2 hands. He's massive compared to Buzby."

"Don't be silly, of course you can. He's an angel, he'll carry you round."

Cross-country practice was starting in five minutes and Rocket was tacked up, observing me with a mild gaze. He was a chestnut with a zigzag blaze down his nose and one white sock. He was the best pony in the riding school. It was like upgrading to a Rolls Royce after riding Buzby who was only 12.2 hands. Despite my nerves I felt a tremor of excitement.

"But it's not right for you not to ride," I said for the hundredth time. Sophie gave me a stern look and prepared to hoist me up into the saddle.

I glanced back at Buzby's stable, only to see him stuffing himself with hay, not minding in the least. "OK," I squeaked. "I'll give it a go."

Rocket stood beautifully as I gathered up the reins and felt for the stirrups. The Six Pack were waiting in a line: Kate on Archie, Rachel on Rusty,

Steph on Monty and Jodie on Minstrel. I hadn't realized just how much I'd missed being part of the gang. We all clunked our crops together and doubled up into pairs to ride down to the wood.

Guy was waiting by the gate, his thoughts obviously elsewhere. "Has anybody seen Ebony and Cindy?" His voice was tight. Everyone shook their heads and I avoided his eyes by focusing on Rocket's rubber reins.

"He's fantastic," I whispered to Sophie as we walked towards the first few rustic jumps. Unlike Buz, Rocket didn't snatch at the reins and try to pull me out of the saddle. I could concentrate on sitting up straight and using my legs to best effect.

"Now remember," Sophie instructed, "he doesn't like to be rushed into a jump and you must give him his head. He'll do the rest."

Guy started off over some low jumps, straw bales and a palisade followed by a slip rail. I was the second to go and felt my heart lurch as I pushed Rocket forward. Everybody was watching. "Please don't let me down," I whispered into Rocket's floppy ears.

Rocket saw the jump ahead and lengthened his stride. I closed my eyes and held my breath. He cleared it effortlessly and automatically turned for the next. I pulled up gasping for breath and flung my arms round Rocket's neck.

"Well done," Guy shouted and then set the next rider off.

I jogged back to Sophie on cloud nine. "He's incredible," I shrieked. "He just flies them."

We had to wait for ages before it was our turn again. Guy moved on to a small ditch with a log over the top which is called a Trakehner, then two banks which you had to step up, and a mini-coffin which Buzby had always refused point blank to jump. A coffin is a jump down to a ditch followed by a jump uphill. It filled me with terror.

"Rocket could jump it in his sleep," Sophie whispered.

But that was without me bouncing around on his back and hindering him.

Jodie made it look easy and Steph went too fast but was still clear. Three of the other riders had refusals.

"OK, Emma, your turn."

I trotted Rocket forward and then circled.

"Look up, look up, look up . . ." I said to myself as I rode down to the Trakehner in a shaky line remembering that you mustn't look in the ditch but straight ahead at the top part of the jump. Rocket ignored my aid to go faster, jumping out of his stride and giving it a wide berth.

"Good boy, brilliant boy!" I patted his neck, ecstatic with pleasure. He popped up the banks as

93

nimble as a cat. It was incredible. I felt like a professional. I had to remind myself to breathe and hastily took in gulps of air.

The coffin was next. I looked across to find my line and that's when the dizziness hit me. The ground wouldn't stay still, everything was reeling. Rocket eased back to a trot, sensing something was wrong and I slumped forward over his neck. I could feel myself slipping helplessly to one side and grabbed at a chunk of mane. Somebody was running towards me, but I couldn't hang on.

The ground was whizzing towards me and I knew it was just seconds before I'd hit it. I remembered thinking that I was falling off wrong, that I should have rolled away from Rocket's hoofs in a tight ball. And then a wave of blackness swamped me and I passed out before I crashed to the ground.

"You fainted." I recognized Sophie among the blur of faces. They were all pressing down, anxious and tense. I struggled up on my elbow and blinked hard. There was a huge grass stain all down one side of my jodhpurs and a rip across the knee.

"OK everyone, move back, give her some air." Guy shuffled forward. "Now Emma, I want you to tell me how many fingers I'm holding up."

I blinked again and did as I was told on automatic pilot.

"And what's your name and address?"

I told him and screwed up my face in confusion.

"I'm checking for concussion, Emma. Do you think you could get to your feet?"

Guy and Sophie walked me back to the stables with Kate leading Rocket from Archie. The cross-country practice was postponed for the day. I just concentrated on putting one foot in front of the other, feeling as weak as a kitten.

Once in the office, Guy said he must ring my parents. I didn't appear to have concussion but I'd certainly have to go home and rest.

"But I know what's wrong with her," Sophie blurted out, gripping the back of a chair.

Guy turned round in surprise.

"She's been secretly dieting." Sophie glanced at me, aching for forgiveness for telling. "She's hardly eaten anything for days. I should have said something but I didn't know how."

My face flushed to a deep crimson.

"Is this true, Emma? When was the last time you had something to eat?"

Mum arrived to pick me up twenty minutes later, her face creased with worry. We sat in silence all the way home finding it too awkward to talk.

"Why Emma, you've always had such a good appetite," Mum burst out as soon as we got into the house. "This is my fault, I'm your mother, I should know when you're upset."

"But you weren't to know." I rushed across the room and flung my arms round her waist. "I've been really stupid," I said, my mouth crumpling with emotion, "I thought I was getting too fat to ride. I didn't realize not eating for a few days would make me ill. I know I've been really stupid."

We clung to each other, really close, and ended up laughing as Mum pushed my hair back off my forehead and picked out bits of straw.

"Oh Emma, you're such a lovely, healthy girl. How did you ever get it in your head that you were overweight?"

The Six Pack arrived in force at 4.30 armed with bags of Mini-Mars Bars, crisps, a tub of chocolate chip ice cream and a packet of cashew nuts.

"It all adds up to over four thousand calories," Steph boasted as Mum pulled a face and praised the virtues of wholesome home cooking. We piled into my bedroom and ripped open the bag of Mars Bars.

"From now on people can take me as they find me," I said grinning, and decided that chocolate had never tasted so good. "It's what's inside a person that counts. I'm never going to be so stupid again."

"We're glad to hear it." Kate wagged a finger. "The Six Pack is not for the faint-hearted." I laughed and threw my chocolate wrapper at her.

"How did you know?" I whispered to Sophie when the others went down to fetch soft drinks.

Sophie crinkled her nose. "I think it was when I caught you throwing a sausage roll out of the saloon window that I realized something was up."

I smiled, feeling slightly embarassed. "I've been a fool," I said. "But I've learnt my lesson."

"We've got something important to tell you," announced Rachel as she came back in the room followed by Steph balancing two drinks in one hand.

Everyone found a seat apart from Jodie who was holding Mickey in the palm of her hand.

"After you left, Cindy came back on Ebby," said Kate. "She'd been out two and a half hours and Ebby was exhausted. And she was in terrible pain with her arthritis."

"Sandra could hardly get her in the stable," Rachel added.

"Guy went mad saying that she should only have been walking and trotting. Anyway Cindy started shouting back and Mrs Brentford came out and nearly had a fit when she saw Ebony Jane. She said that no horse should go out unsupervised and that Guy had better start looking for another job

97

– he obviously didn't care enough about the riding school horses."

"Wow," I mumbled, wishing I hadn't missed all the drama.

"And then," said Steph taking over the story, "Kate and I went into the office and told Guy that unless he started listening to you about Panda, the Six Pack were going on strike. There'd be no more help at weekends and holidays."

I flinched in surprise, twisting the duvet in my fingers. I was all too aware that there were hundreds of girls who'd love to step into our shoes. I could see Jodie thinking the same thing. Also, we were supposed to vote on important decisions. It was another case of Kate taking over if she was given half a chance.

"What did Guy say?" I ventured delicately.

"Nothing," Steph answered. "He just stared at us with his head in his hands."

Dad came home from work at 5.43 exactly. I knew because I was counting the minutes on my digital alarm clock. And I also knew that at this precise moment Mum would be telling him about me falling off Rocket.

I heard raised voices and clapped my hands over my ears. Then I decided that was being childish. I was desperately wondering what to do when the doorbell rang and Mum went to answer it. It was probably someone collecting for a charity or the boys from next door to say their football had gone into our garden.

"Hello. Mrs Parker?" The deep, controlled voice was unmistakeable. "I'm Guy Marshall. I teach your daughter at the riding school."

They went into the sitting room and I waited to be called down, but nothing happened. I paced back and forth wondering what on earth was going on. Guy must be here to talk about me falling off. It was the only explanation . . . Or to say I wasn't welcome at the riding school any more.

I sneaked halfway down the stairs and crouched, listening, but they'd moved into the kitchen and all I could hear was muffled voices. I was convinced it was something bad.

After what seemed like a lifetime the front door opened and shut and I heard Guy leaving down the front path. He hadn't even wanted to see me.

I was desperate to find out what he'd said but a dark feeling of gloom kept me in my bedroom. After a few minutes of silence I heard Mum and Dad on the stairs.

"Can we come in?" Dad peered in awkwardly and they both came across and sat on the edge of the bed.

"That was your riding instructor," Mum said

tentatively. "He told us about this Craig boy who's been calling you names."

"Oh," I mumbled, not knowing what was coming next.

"But we'll talk about that later," said Dad quickly, a twinkle in his eye. "Mr Marshall was here to tell us how much your riding has improved."

My mouth dropped open in sheer surprise.

"It seems you're a bit of a star," he added, grinning. "What's this about winning rosettes and not telling us?"

I glanced to where the orange rosettes were slung on my dressing table. "I've had other things on my mind," I said truthfully.

Dad laughed, thinking I was cracking a joke, and then grew more serious. "We're really proud of you, Emma. Neither of us had any idea how seriously you take your riding." He touched my head softly.

"Thanks, Dad."

"You've grown up a lot, Emma, and we've both decided to support you with your riding as much as possible."

Mum nodded, a tear sliding down her cheek. She always got emotional at important moments.

"We want you to do this cross-country and

100

enjoy every minute of it. If you don't do very well it doesn't matter – it's the trying that counts."

"Maybe we could be your grooms or something," Mum said. "Anything to help." I giggled, remembering that last time Mum had gone near Buzby he'd grabbed hold of her coat and wouldn't let go.

As they closed the door, reminding me that *Animal Kingdom* was about to start on telly, I felt a warm, fizzy happiness rushing through me. They may not be my biological parents, but they were the best Mum and Dad in the whole world.

Chapter Ten

"I can't help it, I can't stop them shaking." I glanced down at my hands which were quivering like two jellies. I'd never known fear like this: I was petrified.

"If this is what cross-country does to you, I'll stick to flatwork," groaned Kate as she came out of the toilet for the third time looking dishcloth grey. She'd only recently started jumping Archie and before that she used to make up any excuse to avoid jumping. "I don't mind telling you, I'm a nervous wreck." She sat down on the stone manger and put her head between her knees.

"Where's Steph?" Sophie rushed up carrying a pile of back protectors. Monty's grey head was sticking out over his stable door, trailing hay. "All of the Six Pack follow on after one another. Jodie's already warming up Minstrel. Come on, you guys, get a move on!"

Guy had rigged up a commentary system with a loudspeaker which kept everyone informed of what was happening. Kate and I agreed this was just going to make it extra-embarrassing when we fell off.

Mum had cooked me a massive breakfast which was sitting in my stomach like a layer of lead. Mum and Dad had set up their fold-up seats by the coffin which just made me doubly nervous. The professional photographer had arrived and moved his equipment to the water jump. There were fourteen ponies competing and as many sets of parents walking round and getting in the way.

"OK, let's strut our stuff." Kate pushed Archie forward. I mounted Rocket and gathered up my reins, trying to send him calming vibes. His back was as tense as an ironing board.

So far only two people out of seven had gone clear. There was also a timed section which Sandra was supposed to be monitoring with a stopwatch.

Rachel was walking Rusty round near the start, keeping him alert. Considering she hadn't been riding for very long she had a really neat position. Suddenly I felt like a sack of potatoes.

Minstrel was the first to set off. Jodie touched him lightly and immediately he started cantering on the spot, snorting through wide nostrils.

Rocket observed everything with a look of superiority. He felt as solid as a table and I'd convinced myself his extra-height would just make the fences look smaller.

Minstrel scorched off, Jodie grabbing hold of him and anchoring him back, not daring to go at more than a steady canter. Rachel moved Rusty up. As he was the oldest pony in the riding school she was just going to do half the course and no jumps over two foot six.

Kate was following Rachel and then it was me. I patted Rocket's neck and asked him to look after me. I tried to visualize the course; straw bales, palisade, tyres, parallel, chair, banks, coffin, water, slip rail, tiger trap, Trakehner, telegraph poles. Home.

"Good luck," called Rachel as she set off at a trot. Archie lined up, his eyes squinting, no doubt thinking up some mischief. Kate tapped him with her heels as a warning to behave.

"Three, two, one . . . Go. Good luck."

I jerked upright, swamped with nerves as Archie thundered off.

"Emma!" I suddenly registered Craig's voice. He was leaning over a rope on Foxy, his face tight and drawn. I scowled at him, warning him not to ruin my moment, angry that he'd already broken my concentration.

"Did you get the letter?" he asked. "I left it in your grooming box."

"What?" I shouted, convinced he was deliberately winding me up.

104

"The letter, it's important. About Panda."

My brain whirred but the cross-country was the only thing I could think of.

"If you'd like to step forward . . ."

Rocket gnawed at the bit, anticipation building up.

"Three, two, one . . . Go!" Rocket shot forward, living up to his name.

I grabbed at the reins and leaned foward, trying to remember everything Guy had taught me. Rocket surged over the bales and palisade as if they were nothing. We stood off for the tyres effortlessly and I started to relax and enjoy myself. It was the most incredible feeling of power and freedom. Riding a proper course was so different from schooling over one jump at a time.

We turned into the woods for the chair, fighting back to a slower canter.

"Stop!" Suddenly Sandra appeared from among the trees and blew on a whistle, making Rocket swerve to one side. Luckily his head came up and threw me back into the saddle.

"Archie's playing up," Sandra shouted. "You'll have to wait."

I spotted Archie's solid, immovable bulk in the trees, refusing at the chair. Kate was pulling at the reins trying to upset his balance. She yelled and kicked and suddenly Archie flung himself over the fence and charged on to the next as if he hadn't made any fuss at all. A great whoop of delight went up from the parents who had converged round the jumps.

"This is the timed section," said Sandra patting Rocket. "I'll set the stopwatch and say go."

Suddenly I knew I was going to go as fast as I could. I was going to give it my all. Rocket bristled, bunching his muscles. We were united in one purpose – winning . . .

We soared over the chair, checked back for the steps and balanced up for the coffin. I leaned back and made Rocket bounce into it just as Guy had told us. I'd never been so determined to clear anything in my life. My legs were set like concrete.

Rocket didn't hesitate once. I saw Mum and Dad in a blur and then I was leaping out over the other side. Clear!

We eased back after the timed section and that's when I made my first mistake. My legs went slack as I entered the water and Rocket pecked on landing, sending me sprawling onto his neck. Water shot up into my mouth and eyes and I lost my line. We brushed against a tree, my stirrup crashing into the bark. Amazingly, I stayed on board and rode like a Trojan over the slip rail and tiger trap. By the telegraph poles I knew we'd cracked it and wanted to thrust my fist in the air like Frankie Dettori. Sophie was waiting at the finish, jumping up and down on the spot, hugging herself.

I'd done it. I'd gone clear and fast on a strange pony and proved to myself and everyone else that I could ride. I wanted to keep the happiness inside me for ever.

"That was brilliant!" Sophie gave me a bear-hug that would have knocked the breath out of a sumo wrestler.

I jumped off Rocket and loosened his girth, ready to walk him round and cool off. Mum and Dad came across in a flurry of excitement, patting and fussing over Rocket as if he were their own.

"Thanks," I whispered to Sophie, "for everything."

It was ages before I was able to break away from everybody and lead Rocket back to the stables. Guy announced on the loudspeaker that the last rider was on the course and had fallen off at the water. I was sure it was Craig.

Sandra was walking towards me leading Panda who was all tacked up with protective boots and a martingale. "Guy's popping her round the course now everyone's finished," she mumbled, looking bored. "I suppose her snotty owner will be turning up soon. She's got some nerve after yesterday."

I decided to give Ebony Jane an extra carrot and

some fuss. Then it hit me like a thunderbolt – what Craig had said about a letter.

I searched through my grooming box and found the envelope under the hoof-oil tin.

Dear Emma,
I'm truly sorry for the way I've treated you. I couldn't face the idea of a girl pen pal being a better rider than me. Unfortunately it was me who left the pitchfork in the stable and the lid off the feed bin. I've learnt my lesson about pranks. The only person they hurt is yourself. I should have told you about Cindy being my cousin and I should have told you about Panda. She has some kind of breathing disorder caused by the spores in hay and straw – obstructive pulmonary disease or something. It's also known as broken wind. Please don't let Guy buy her – he's being ripped off.
    Craig.

I was running flat out across the field, my lungs burning and my arms flailing. Guy was walking Panda round near the start. If I took a short cut through the wood I could block them as they approached the first fence. It was my only option.

Bright green nettles stung at my bare arms as I ran through the undergrowth, tripping and nearly falling. I could hardly get my breath now, it was coming in shallow bursts. This was how Panda must feel, I realized with dread, and forced my legs on, climbing the last bank on my hands and knees.

I was too late. I could see Panda's golden body glimmering between the trees – she was already on the course. I had to do something. In one last desperate attempt I levered myself up and ran out in front of the first jump. As I turned to position myself all I could see in the dim light was Panda's legs hurtling towards me.

"Watch out!" Guy's startled voice seemed to tear out of his throat. Panda slammed in her heels at the last minute, scuffing up the loose sandy earth and throwing her off balance. Her near shoulder crashed into my body, tossing me to one side like a feather-light pillow.

Intense, stinging pain shot across my chest as the breath was knocked out of me. But it didn't matter. I'd stopped Panda. She was staring at me with a look of concern in her huge liquid eyes. All I had to do now was explain why.

During the next hour things took a bizarre turn. Amid the confusion Cindy turned up, but not alone. She was accompanied by the instantly recognizable vet from *Animal Kingdom* who was shooting thunderous looks at her.

There was a wave of excitement at the presence

of a famous person but it passed me by. I'd learnt that if someone was famous it didn't mean they were automatically nice. You had to judge people on what they were and not who they were.

We learnt a lot about Panda's illness. It was the dust in hay and straw which caused her to cough and made her short of breath. The double breathing was an effort to get more air into her lungs. Panda only suffered mild symptoms of the disease which was why it had passed unnoticed by so many people. However it still meant she wasn't a hundred per cent sound or capable of galloping and cross-country.

Cindy had known this all the time. She'd deliberately tried to con Guy after Craig had told her about my letters and about an up-and-coming showjumper and riding instructor who was looking for good horses.

The vet from *Animal Kingdom* was her fiancé and unknowingly he'd signed a piece of paper which he'd thought was just a form from the newsagent's, but which turned out to be a veterinary certificate which Cindy had taken from his files. As soon as he'd found out, he'd made every effort to track her down.

"You've not only lost your fiancé," he spat at her, "you've lost the only real friend you had. Don't bother giving me back the ring."

They left in silence, with a wall of bitterness between them. Even Cindy had enough of a conscience to look shamefaced.

Guy was devastated and walked quietly down to the office, shutting himself in. He'd been so obsessed with Panda, so blinded by her good nature and talent, that he hadn't looked at the whole picture. The tell-tale signs had always been there but he'd chosen not to see them.

While everybody was talking non-stop and repeating the facts over and over again, I sneaked back to the stables with one clear purpose. Pulling out some carrots from my coat pocket I went first to Rocket's stable and thanked him for the day. Then I went to Ebony Jane, gave her bony neck a good pat and blew up her nostrils which she loved. inally I went to Buzby, pulling open his stable door and going in, wrapping my arms round his thick, strong neck until I was covered in grey hairs from head to foot.

"Dear, darling Buz, thank you for teaching mc to ride." He eyed me with a look of disapproval, until I fished out his favourite sweets, liquorice allsorts, and he ate them happily from my open hand.

"Even when I outgrow you, I'll never forget you," I whispered into his woolly ears while he slurped away happily. "You're not fast and you're not showy but it doesn't matter because you've got an elephant-sized personality." He glared at me for being soppy but I carried on.

"Horses always make the best listeners." Guy appeared in the doorway, his face strained but smiling.

I jumped slightly, feeling a prickle of embarrassment. "What will happen to Panda?" I blurted out with a need to know.

Guy shrugged. "She'll be put on woodshavings and given dust-free hay and six weeks rest, then she'll probably become a show horse or a brood mare. The good news is Mrs Brentford has agreed to keep her here and find a suitable home for her when she's better."

"That's brillant!" I perked up, genuinely thrilled. Panda was a top horse and deserved the best.

"I guess we've all made a few mistakes this week." Guy studied his feet. It was his turn to be embarrassed.

"My mum says it's not how many mistakes we make but whether we learn from them that counts."

Guy nodded, understanding. "I'm going to keep working here so you'll have to put up with my bad temper a little longer."

"I think the Six Pack can cope with that," I said grinning.

"Oh here, I nearly forgot." He brought his hands out from behind his back and passed me a beautiful crystal horse engraved with the words, "Brook House Riding School Pony Week. Most Improved Rider."

I swallowed hard not knowing what to say. I clutched the statue as if I was holding something rare and priceless.

"You've earned it, although at the beginning of the week I would have sworn you were a 200–1 outsider."

"So would I," I laughed, marvelling at the way things could change. "It just proves that where there's life, there's hope." I fingered the delicate glass in awe. "If at first you don't succeed, try, try, try again. But most important of all, more than anything – *believe in yourself*!"

Answers to the Quiz in Chapter Eight

When is a Thoroughbred's official birthday?
　1st January.

What was the name of the first mare to win the Hickstead Derby?
　Bluebird.

Which brush should be used on a pony's mane and tail?
　A body brush.

Most greys are born black or brown. True or false?
　True.

A Falabella is the smallest breed of horse. True or false?
　True.

What is a gag?
　A bit with leather straps running through the bit cheeks. Useful for a strong horse.

How would you describe a Trakehner?
A cross-country jump with a log suspended over a ditch.

All ponies should be fed immediately before being ridden. True or False?
False.

The poll is to be found on which part of the horse's body?
The top of the head, behind the ears.

What are the symptoms of strangles?
Thick discharge from the nose, a high temperature, coughing, and a typical stance where the neck is extended and the nose poking out.

A Palomino is recognized as a breed in America, but elsewhere is only classed as a colour. True or False?
True.

How many inches in a hand?
Four.

What is a skewbald?
A horse or pony with brown and white patches.

Is ragwort a poisonous plant?
Yes.

On which side should you plait up a horse's mane?
    The right side.

From which side should you lead a pony?
    The left side.

What is laminitis caused by?
    Usually by too much rich grass or by hard feed.

Samantha Alexander
Riding School 1: Jodie

Six very different girls – Jodie, Emma, Steph, Kate, Sophie and Rachel – bound together by their passion for horses.

A crazy horse and a girl with a smashed leg and no courage. What a winning pair. The only thing Minstrel and I had in common was our hang-ups. And that wasn't nearly enough to win at the Brook House Annual Show . . .

Jodie Williams hasn't been near a horse for two years since the accident which left her with a shattered leg. It takes an Arab stallion and a new group of friends to get her back in the saddle.

Samantha Alexander
Hollywell Stables 1: Flying Start

Hollywell Stables – sanctuary for horses and ponies. It was a dream come true for Mel, Ross and Katie . . .

A mysterious note led them to Queenie, neglected and desperately hungry, imprisoned in a scrapyard. Rescuing Colorado was much more complicated. The spirited Mustang terrified his wealthy owner: her solution was to have him destroyed.

But for every lucky horse at the sanctuary there are so many others in desperate need of rescue. And money is running out fast.

Praise for Hollywell Stables:

'Hollywell Stables is the vanguard of the new breed of pony stories . . . these are cracking stories.' *TES*

'The action comes thick and fast with adventure after adventure rolling off each page.' *Riding Magazine*

Samantha Alexander
Riders 1: Will to Win

"Alex Johnson, I'll never understand you. You own a horse with a reputation for being a complete maniac and you think you can waltz into your first competition and win."

"I don't think," I threw back at her. "I know."

Alex Johnson is a girl with one burning ambition: to become a champion three-day eventer. The only thing distracting her from her goal is the gorgeous Ash Burgess, who runs the yard where she keeps her horse . . .

A selected list of SAMANTHA ALEXANDER books available from Macmillan

The prices shown below are correct at the time of going to press. However, Macmillan Publishers reserve the right to show new retail prices on covers which may differ from those previously advertised.

RIDING SCHOOL

1.	Jodie	0 330 36836 2	£2.99
2.	Emma	0 330 36837 0	£2.99
3.	Steph	0 330 36838 9	£2.99
4.	Kate	0 330 36839 7	£2.99
5.	Sophie	0 330 36840 0	£2.99
6.	Rachel	0 330 36841 9	£2.99

HOLLYWELL STABLES

1.	Flying Start	0 330 33639 8	£2.99
2.	The Gamble	0 330 33685 1	£2.99
3.	The Chase	0 330 33857 9	£2.99
4.	Fame	0 330 33858 7	£2.99
5.	The Mission	0 330 34199 5	£2.99
6.	Trapped	0 330 34200 2	£2.99
7.	Running Wild	0 330 34201 0	£2.99
8.	Secrets	0 330 34202 9	£2.99